MIDDLE SCHOOL

FROM HERO TO ZERO

MIDDLE SCHOOL

FROM HERO TO ZERO

JAMES PATTERSON

AND CHRIS TEBBETTS

ILLUSTRATED BY LAURA PARK

LITTLE, BROWN AND COMPANY

NEW YORK • BOSTON • LONDON

JIMMY Patterson Books / Little, Brown and Company
Hachette Book Group
1290 Avenue of the Americas, New York, NY 10104
jimmypatterson.org

First Edition: March 2018

JIMMY Patterson Books is an imprint of Little, Brown and Company, a division of Hachette Book Group, Inc. The Little, Brown name and logo are trademarks of Hachette Book Group, Inc. The JIMMY Patterson® name and logo are trademarks of JBP Business, LLC.

Middle School® is a trademark of JBP Business, LLC.

The publisher is not responsible for websites (or their content) that are not owned by the publisher.

The Hachette Speakers Bureau provides a wide range of authors for speaking events. To find out more, go to hachettespeakersbureau.com or call (866) 376-6591.

Library of Congress Cataloging-in-Publication Data
Names: Patterson, James, author. | Tebbetts, Christopher, author. | Park, Laura, illustrator.
Title: From hero to zero / James Patterson, Chris Tebbetts ; illustrated by Laura Park.
Description: New York : Little, Brown and Company, 2018 | Series: Middle school ; 10 | "Jimmy Patterson Books." | Summary: "Rafe Khatchadorian takes his troublemaking ways across the pond and gets lost in London!"— Provided by publisher.
Identifiers: LCCN 2016049224 | ISBN 978-0-316-34690-0 (paper over board) | ISBN 978-0-316-44898-7 (Scholastic ed.)

10 9 8 7 6 5 4 3

LSC-C

Printed in the United States of America

Hi, I'm JIMMY!

Like me, you probably noticed the world is run by adults.

But ask yourself: Who would do the best job of making books that *kids* will love?

Yeah. **Kids!**

So that's how the idea of JIMMY books came to life.

We want every JIMMY book to be so good that when you're finished, you'll say,

"PLEASE GIVE ME ANOTHER BOOK!"

Give this one a try and see if you agree.

(If not, you're probably an adult!)

JIMMY PATTERSON BOOKS FOR YOUNG READERS

James Patterson Presents

Sci-Fi Junior High by John Martin and Scott Seegert

Sci-Fi Junior High: Crash Landing by John Martin and Scott Seegert

How to Be a Supervillain by Michael Fry

How to Be a Supervillain: Born to Be Good by Michael Fry

The Unflushables by Ron Bates

The Middle School Series by James Patterson

Middle School: The Worst Years of My Life

Middle School: Get Me Out of Here!

Middle School: Big Fat Liar

Middle School: How I Survived Bullies, Broccoli, and Snake Hill

Middle School: Ultimate Showdown

Middle School: Save Rafe!

Middle School: Just My Rotten Luck

Middle School: Dog's Best Friend

Middle School: Escape to Australia

Middle School: From Hero to Zero

The I Funny Series by James Patterson

I Funny

I Even Funnier

I Totally Funniest

I Funny TV

I Funny: School of Laughs

I Funny: Around the World

The Treasure Hunters Series by James Patterson

Treasure Hunters

Treasure Hunters: Danger Down the Nile

Treasure Hunters: Secret of the Forbidden City

Treasure Hunters: Peril at the Top of the World

Treasure Hunters: Quest for the City of Gold

The House of Robots Series by James Patterson

House of Robots

House of Robots: Robots Go Wild!

House of Robots: Robot Revolution

The Daniel X Series by James Patterson

The Dangerous Days of Daniel X

Daniel X: Watch the Skies

Daniel X: Demons and Druids

Daniel X: Game Over

Daniel X: Armageddon

Daniel X: Lights Out

Other Illustrated Novels and Stories

Laugh Out Loud

Pottymouth and Stoopid

Jacky Ha-Ha

Jacky Ha-Ha: My Life Is a Joke

Public School Superhero

Word of Mouse

Give Please a Chance

Give Thank You a Try

Big Words for Little Geniuses

The Candies Save Christmas

For exclusives, trailers, and other information, visit jimmypatterson.org.

This one goes out to
the Londonderrys:
Barbara, Jan, Joe,
Ruth, and Vicki
—C.T.

CHAPTER 1

PACKING UP

•REC
Hi, everyone. It's me, Rafe! I don't have a lot of time, because in about five minutes I have to get in the car... to go to the airport... to get on a plane... to fly to London.
Yes, that London. The big one in England. It's a school trip, and we're going to be seeing all kinds of Englishy stuff, like Buckingham Palace, the Tower of London, the modern art museu and the London Eye, which is like a Ferris wheel made out of space stations on steroids. I'm crazy excited!
•REC

But you want to know what's even crazier?
•REC
I am SO **NOT PACKED!** And did I mention that I'm leaving in five minutes? Here's what I have so far.

•REC
One very empty suitcase...

And way over here: one pile of clothes, shoes, and bathroom stuff. I don't care what I wear in London, as long as I can change my underwear every day. And I need comfortable shoes, too. My art teacher, Ms. Donatello, said we're going to be walking our butts off over there. (Well, she didn't really say "butts off.")

My mom gave me fifty pounds of spending money. But that's just what they call money over there, it's not like fifty actual pounds of money. It's more like fifty dollars—but I'll take it! Thanks, Mom!

I think I made a wrong turn...
Don't forget to pack!
•REC

If you know me, you know I never go anywhere without my sketchbook. I like to draw as much as I like to eat. Which, by the way, is a lot.

And I'm borrowing my grandma's phone, too, so I can keep making these videos. Everyone on the trip has to do a report on it, and mine's going to be full-on multimedia, with video, drawing, writing, and I don't even know what else. I guess I'll find out when I get there.

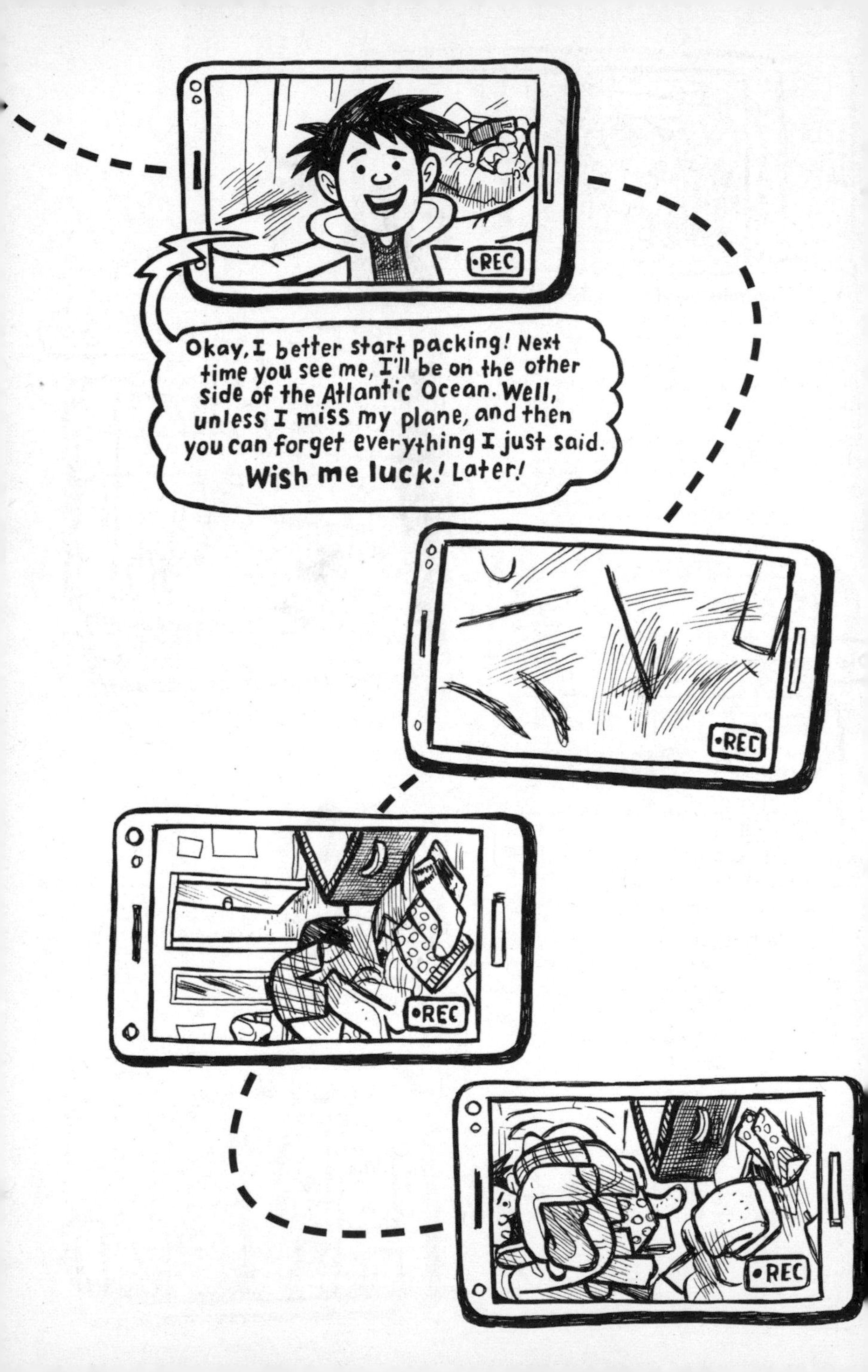
•REC
Okay, I better start packing! Next time you see me, I'll be on the other side of the Atlantic Ocean. Well, unless I miss my plane, and then you can forget everything I just said. Wish me luck! Later!
•REC
•REC
•REC

•REC
Rafe? Mom said you have to leave now.
•REC
Coming!
Did you remember everything?
•REC
Yes, I remembered everything. Now stay out of my room!
•REC

•REC
What an idiot.
•REC
REC
Seriously, Rafe? You're already losing things. This trip is going to be one big disaster. I could be wrong, but let's face it, big brother: you're the king of disasters. So, good luck—you're going to need it. And watch out, London, because here comes Rafe!
Click!

CHAPTER 2

TIME TO GO

At the airport, everything was crazy. There were kids and parents and chaperones trying to find each other, plus half a zillion other people, all traveling in half a zillion other directions.

And then there was a little room where we could all finally stop and gather up for our big goodbyes before I had to find the other kids. It was definitely insane, but I could actually start to see the adventure I had been imagining.

"Excited?" Grandma asked me.

"Yep," I said, but honestly, I was kind of nervous, too.

"You sure you have everything?" Mom asked me.

"Yep," I said, even though I had this weird feeling I was forgetting something.

"Are you *really* sure you have everything?" Georgia asked, in that annoying way where you know she's not *really* asking a question. Then she held up the phone Grandma was lending me for the trip with a really smug smile.

"Where'd you get that?" I asked her.

"It was sitting on your bed while you were walking out the front door, genius," she said.

"I told you to stay out of my room," I said, and grabbed it back.

When it comes to snooping, my sister has superpowers. And she was definitely going to do some supersnooping while I was in London. That's why I'd spent the last week blowing my nose and leaving all the used Kleenex in my desk and dresser drawers. There was also some mega-realistic plastic dog puke on my closet floor, and a note under my mattress that said "STOP SNOOPING OR DIE!"

But that was it. I couldn't worry about Georgia anymore. It was time to go. Mrs. Stricker was yelling at the parents to say goodbye so we could all get ready to hop into the security line, which looked about two miles long.

"All right, off you go," Mom said, and then walked me a little closer. When it comes to saying goodbye, Mom always likes a little time alone with me. I kind of like it, too.

"This is so exciting. Your first time out of the country without me!" she said. "And who would've thought you'd turn into such an international jetsetter? I thought Australia was exciting enough, what with the surfing and drop bears and the bunyip adventure, which I would personally rather forget." She stopped, embarrassed.

She was rambling about my last trip abroad—I won a school art competition and the prize was a free trip to the Land Down Under. Things didn't turn out so well, but I was glad I had the chance to go.

Even if it did end in disaster.

"You're going to have a great trip, sweetheart," Mom finished.

"Yeah...," I said. "I guess so."

"You guess?" Mom said.

"Well..."

"What is it?" she said.

She can always tell when I'm feeling weird about something. And this wasn't the kind of weird I wanted to put in a video, where everyone would hear about it. But I could tell Mom, even if it came out a little awkward.

See, this was supposed to be some great thing, right? I was really lucky to go somewhere as crazy exciting as London. (Grandma helped out and got her friends to buy about twenty thousand rolls of wrapping paper in our school fund-raiser, and I got a scholarship, thanks to Ms. Donatello.)

But here's the problem: the only real friends I had were staying back in Hills Village, on the wrong side of a pretty huge ocean. That included Flip Savage, the funniest kid I've ever known, and Junior, my dog and best non-human friend.

In other words, I was on my own for this trip. *Totally friend-free*. Which was like going back to the bad old days at Hills Village Middle School, when I was about as popular as Mystery Meat Monday in the cafeteria.

"It's just...I don't have any friends on this trip," I told Mom.

"What about Jeanne Galletta?" Mom asked.

"Jeanne doesn't count," I said. "She's really nice, but it's not like we're actually friends."

I probably (definitely) wasn't supposed to like Jeanne as much as I did. But try telling that to my brain. I just couldn't help it.

Right now, Jeanne was standing with the rest of the kids along with her stupid perfect boyfriend, Jared McCall, who I am NOT jealous of. It's just that Jared's so good at everything, you kind of want to stick his head in a toilet sometimes.

"Well, I see at least one girl looking your way, Rafe. I think you might be more popular with the ladies than you realize."

"Don't say *ladies,*" I said. "And besides, you're my mom. You have to say that stuff."

"How about Ms. Donatello?" Mom said. "You like her, don't you?"

"Sure," I said. "For a teacher. But that doesn't really count."

"Well, here's an idea. Why don't you try making a few *new* friends?" Mom asked me.

That one was harder to answer. I mean, everyone in middle school already knew me, and it wasn't like I'd been sitting on all the good parts of my personality so I could bust them out now and start winning popularity contests. I pretty much knew by now who my friends were and *who wouldn't be caught dead talking to me*.

I didn't know if Mom would understand all that, but I'll bet you do, right?

"I guess," I mumbled, which was easier than telling her everything I just told you.

"It can't hurt to be friendly," Mom said. "I

wouldn't want you to spend the whole trip alone with that sketchbook of yours."

She had a point. I did bring my sketchbook, for sure. I love to draw, including my Loozer comics, which you may already know about. You'll definitely see some more of those later.

"Now, you better go or Mrs. Stricker is going to leave without you," she said.

Mrs. Stricker is the principal of Hills Village Middle School. She also happens to hate the ground I walk on. Right now, she was evil-eyeing me like I was holding up the whole airport.

"Sorry, Ida," Mom called out to her. "He's coming!"

"Mmglrrr," Mrs. Stricker mumbled, which I think was something about *should have left without him.* But I couldn't be sure.

"Bon voyage, sweetie!" Mom said, and gave me one more quick hug for luck. "I love you. And remember what I said."

"I will," I told her.

And I would.

I'd remember every word...just as soon as I got busy being the *least* popular kid on that whole trip.

Hey, it's a tough job, but someone has to do it.

100%
ROCK STAR
THIS SPACE RESERVED FOR JEANNE GALLETTA.
90%
President and Captain of EVERYTHING.
80%
Has it made in the shade.
70%
The kind of kid who gets elected class secretary.
60%
Never eats lunch alone.
50%
Enough friends, most of the time.
40%
Life could be WORSE (COULD ALSO BE BETTER.)
30%
At least three friends. Maybe works at the school store.
20%
A friend or two, probably weirdos.
10%
Maybe one friend.
0%
BIG FAT ZERO.
That would be me.
THE POPULARITY SCALE

INTRODUCING DRYDEN

Hang on. Sure I was all set to be pretty lonely and awkward, but you don't even know the *worst* part.

Once everyone said goodbye, Mrs. Stricker and the other chaperones got us all standing in one place and started counting heads.

"We will have four daily roll calls on this trip," Mrs. Stricker said. "When I call your name, respond with a nice, clear 'PRESENT.' Not 'Yeah' or 'Huh?' or 'That's me.' The proper response is 'PRESENT.' Understood?"

And then she started down the list, checking off names in alphabetical order.

"Katrina Anderson?"

"Present!"

"Colin Aziz?"

"Present!"

"Andrea Chin?"

"Yeah! Uh, I mean, present!"

Then all of a sudden, someone was yelling in the airport.

"Excuse me! So sorry! Coming through! Excuse me!"

I looked over and saw this lady running toward us, waving at Mrs. Stricker. Behind her was a man in a suit and tie, carrying a suitcase. They both looked kind of fancy to me, like they belonged on the cover of *Whole-Lotta-Money Magazine*. But I'd never seen them before.

"I'm so terribly sorry to be late," the lady said when she got there. "Dryden is going potty in the little boys' room, but he'll be right here."

"Who's Dryden?" someone said behind me. I was wondering the same thing. Was there some little kid coming on this trip?

"It's almost time for us to be at our gate," Mrs. Stricker said. She had this look on her face like she hadn't gone to the bathroom in a week. I think she was trying to be polite.

"Yes, yes, yes," the lady said. "Again, I'm soooo very sorry, but I can't tell you how much Dryden is looking forward to this. We took him to Hong Kong last summer, and he—"

"Here he is!" the man in the suit said. "Come along, Dryden. Chop-chop!"

"I'm coming, I'm coming. Keep your pants on, Dad," someone said.

When I turned around, I couldn't believe my eyes. Right there, coming toward us, was the one… the only… *Miller.*

A.k.a. Miller the Killer.

Also known as the Grim Reaper in size 10 Nikes, and the last kid on earth I wanted to see just then.

Ever since middle school started, Miller and I had been through a lot of ups and downs. Mostly, it was about me trying to stand *up* for myself and him knocking me back *down*. During football season, when we were on the same team and I was actually useful to him, we had this weird truce, and things were okay for about five minutes. After our last game, Miller went back to spending most of his time making sure I was suffering enough. I guess everyone needs a hobby.

So on top of being obnoxious, mean, and just dumb enough to be dangerous, it turned out Miller was rich, too. And his name was... *Dryden?* Nobody at school ever called him anything but Miller. Not even the teachers. I actually kind of thought his full name was Miller Miller.

Meanwhile, I don't think "Dryden" was nearly as into this trip as his parents were saying. He was standing there now, looking about as excited as an extra-angry cow on the way to the slaughterhouse. And that was lousy news for all of us. Because the only thing worse than regular Miller is Miller in a bad mood.

So far, he hadn't even noticed me. I guess he was too busy sulking. But there were only thirty-six kids in the group. It wasn't like I'd blend in forever. It was just a matter of time before I got on Miller's radar, and then the real fun would begin.

And by *real fun,* I pretty much mean the exact opposite.

HERE

All right then," Mrs. Stricker said, while Miller's parents gave him a bunch of hugs and kisses goodbye (which was also weird to see). "Where was I?"

"Andrea Chin," Alison Prouty said, because she lives to kiss up.

"Present," Andrea said. "Again."

"Martin D'Angelo?" Mrs. Stricker said.

"Present!" Martin said.

And it kept going pretty much like that, up to the *K*s, which is me. I was standing on the edge of the group, trying not to be noticed, but then Mrs. Stricker called my name.

"Rafe Khatchadorian?" she said.

"Present!" I said…sort of. Except my voice

cracked right in the middle of saying it.

My voice had been doing that a lot lately, which my mom told me not to worry too much about, but it's really embarrassing. It just stank that I had to sound like I'd swallowed an old bike horn at completely random times. Especially with thirty-five kids right there to hear it.

A bunch of people laughed, of course. But not as hard as they did after Miller put in his two cents.

"Is that Khatchadorian? Or Squeakadorian?" he yelled, putting a couple fake squeaks of his own in for good measure, and even more people cracked up. I saw Jeanne smile, too, even though she put a hand over her mouth to hide it. At least she was *trying* to be nice.

I didn't even care about Miller's stupid nicknames anymore. He had about a hundred of them, and it had gotten old a long time ago. The problem was, it felt like Miller had just turned on his OPEN FOR BUSINESS sign. When I looked over, he was smiling like maybe this trip wouldn't be so bad after all.

Great. Just great. We weren't even out of the country yet, and I was already wishing I'd never heard of London.

Or Miller, for that matter.

LIVING HISTORY, KA-CHING, KA-CHING!

After that, the chaperones started passing around these blue folders while Mrs. Stricker got up and talked to everybody.

"What you are receiving now are packets for the Living-Learning Report you will be creating here in London as a group," Mrs. Stricker said.

I already knew about the report, but this was a bunch of new information. Those packets were as thick as Snickers bars, and not in a good way.

"On the first page, you will see a list of topics to be included—arts, politics, science, history, and current events," she said.

In other words, Mrs. Stricker was making sure that we put plenty of *school* into this school trip. And she wasn't done yet, either.

"Each of those five topics will have one student coordinator. I will also be assigning one student as the entire project's Editor in Chief. That person will work with me, Ms. Donatello, Mr. Rourke, and the topic leaders to oversee all content you generate as a team."

The whole Editor in Chief thing had Jeanne Galletta's name written all over it. I could see she was already going through that packet like it was Thanksgiving dinner and she couldn't wait to dig in.

"We will be posting updates to the Hills Village Middle School website every day, effectively creating an informational running blog out of our trip," Mrs. Stricker said. "We will also post our final report on Living-Learning-Contest.com, so I expect you all to take this project very seriously."

"Contest?" Andrea Chin said. "What's that mean?"

"It's another word for a competition," Alison Prouty said.

"Duh," Andrea said. "I just mean—"

"Quiet!" Mrs. Stricker yelled, not so quietly. "If you will listen, I will explain."

She gave us the famous Stricker eyeball for

a second. If you've never seen it, believe me, you don't want to. Mrs. Stricker can do more with a single look than most people can do with a laser cannon.

Then she kept going.

“Schools from around the country will be participating in this project. One school will be chosen as the Grand Prize winner and awarded ten thousand dollars’ worth of books and supplies. Also, every member of the winning school’s team will be placed in a drawing for an individual thousand-dollar cash prize.”

I don’t know why Mrs. Stricker waited so long to tell us that part, but here’s what I heard when she said it:

All of a sudden, this trip didn't seem quite as bad as it had a minute ago. Even if my chances of winning that money were a million to one, it was better than not having a chance at all. Even at those odds, it's as close as I've ever come to a thousand bucks before. (At least since my dog-walking empire went out of business.)

So you *know* everyone was paying attention now. And everyone was going to be taking those reports way more seriously now, too.

For that kind of cash, I sure was.

YOU CAN PICK YOUR NOSE, BUT YOU CAN'T PICK YOUR SEAT

The airplane we took to London was HUGE. The seats went so far back, it was basically like a football stadium. Each row had three seats on each side and *five* across the middle, with each section separated by aisles, which just made it look even more like referees were going to sprint out of the cockpit instead of pilots.

It was all assigned, too, so I didn't have a choice. I was next to Bobby Flynn, who was next to Martin D'Angelo, who was next to Kadir Fletcher, who was next to…you guessed it…Miller.

Talk about good news, bad news. It wasn't like Miller was right on top of me. But it did remind me of the first part of my new favorite movie, *Hideous 3*. That's when the "new neighbors" are moving into the house next door, and you just *know* they're flesh-eaters, because...well, you saw the first two *Hideous* movies. So you can't even relax, even though nothing's happened yet, because you know what's coming. First chance they get, those "ordinary" neighbors are going to start chewing people's faces off.

That's basically how I felt with Miller sitting there. We had seven hours to go until we reached London. Plenty of time for the horror show to begin.

At least I had that three-person shield between me and Miller. Bobby, Martin, and Kadir were all best friends. Bobby was going to be my roommate at the hotel in London, partly because I didn't have anyone to room with, and mostly because the three of them drew straws, and Bobby lost. So Martin and Kadir were sharing a room, and Bobby was stuck with me.

Speaking of Bobby, he didn't look very excited to be there, either. Most of the kids around us were yelling and cutting up, but not Bobby. He looked kind of nervous, and already had his seat belt on really tight.

I figured I should at least talk to the kid who had to room with me. That's what Mom would have said. Be friendly, right?

"You okay, Bobby?" I asked.

"Bobby's not so hot on flying," Martin said.

"Shut up," Bobby told him.

"Just don't have a panic attack," Kadir said.

"I'm not!" Bobby said.

I kind of knew how Bobby felt, though. I'm afraid of heights, and the last time I got stuck somewhere really high, I felt the same way he looked right now—like he was wishing he could be *anywhere* else.

"It'll be okay," I said, which sounded lame. But Bobby seemed like he appreciated it.

"Thanks, Rafe," he said.

That was it. Then the three of them went back to talking about how Comic Con in Fort Lauderdale would be the ultimate spring break.

And I started wondering if maybe Mom had a point. It couldn't hurt to be nice to people, right? Maybe if I played it right, I could hang out with Bobby and those guys in London. *Maybe* even make a friend or two while I was over there, I thought.

But that was before the plane took off and everything went so wrong, wrong, wrong, at 40,000 feet over the Atlantic Ocean.

WORST. FLIGHT. EVER.

At first, the flight went okay. I drew in my sketchbook for a while. Then they gave us peanuts and showed the new Avengers movie. After that, it was time for lunch. I got this chicken thing with rice and gravy, since the other choice was fish (gag).

It was right after they handed out the food that things started getting a little bumpy. And then a lot bumpy. Pretty soon, the whole plane was bouncing around like a jeep on an old dirt road.

"What's going on?" Bobby said, starting to freak out a bit.

DING!

The seat belt lights came on then, and one of the crew got onto the intercom.

"Ladies and gentlemen, please be sure you are in your seats with your seat belts securely fastened while we experience a little turbulence."

"A *little* turbulence? What does that mean?" Bobby said. He looked like someone had just told him he had half an hour to live.

"Don't worry about it," Martin told him. "It's just rough air—"

But then we hit a big one—*ba-bump!*

And then a *really* big one—*BA-BUMP!* That one felt like the time my mom drove over a parking block at the grocery store. The brownie that came with my lunch caught a little air off the tray, and I saw an empty Coke can go rolling down the aisle.

By now, Bobby was holding on to the armrests like his hands were made out of superglue. He had his eyes squeezed shut, and he was saying, "Oh no…oh…no…oh no…"

There wasn't much I could do, since I was all buckled in. But I wanted to help Bobby if I could. You know, like a friend would do.

And then I got an idea. One thing I'm good at sometimes is making people laugh. And for this idea, I didn't even have to leave my seat.

So here's what I did: I took the airsick bag out of the little pocket on the seat in front of me. Then I opened it up and dumped the rest of my chicken, rice, and gravy into the bag.

"Hey, Bobby?" I said. "Check it out."

When he looked over, I took a big spoonful out of the barf bag and shoved it in my mouth.

"Mmmm," I said. "Even better the second time around."

And just for the record—I know, I know—it wasn't exactly the smartest joke to pull just then. I can see that *now*. But I'm not exactly a world champion at thinking ahead.

It was supposed to be funny. In fact, it was supposed to be *hilarious* and take Bobby's mind off the turbulence.

Instead, Bobby took one look at me eating glop out of that barf bag, and his eyes got big. His cheeks puffed out and he put a hand over his mouth. By the time I figured out my own mistake, it was too late. The chunks had already started to blow.

Bobby tried to jump up, but his seat belt was

still on tight. It just jammed into his stomach and made everything fly a little farther, if you know what I mean. Some of it got on Kadir. And even worse, some of it got on Miller.

There was a big panic then. People were grossed out and started yelling. Mrs. Stricker was coming up the aisle, and the flight attendant was coming down the aisle, telling Mrs. Stricker to get back to her seat. Bobby was looking like he wanted to cry. Kadir looked like he might be the next one to hurl. (He was.)

And Miller was sitting there with half of Bobby's breakfast on his sweatshirt, staring me down like there was no tomorrow.

Which, for all I knew, there wasn't going to be.

CHAPTER 8

BULLY FOR YOU

So here's a real question.

If you try to do something good and it ends up being something bad instead, what does that make you? A good person or a bad person? Because I wasn't even sure what to think of myself, even if I did know what everyone else thought of me.

Between the glares and the whispers, it was pretty obvious.

Word got around pretty quickly about what happened. Before we even landed in London, I was already more unpopular than I was when we left the United States, which I didn't actually think was possible.

100%
90%
80%
60%
0
President and
EVERYTHING
Has it made in the shade.
kind of kid who gets
secretary.
Never eats
alone
time.
Life could be WORSE.
BE BETTER.
least three frien
Maybe works at the
A friend or two, probably weirdos.
Maybe one friend. Maybe.
BIG FAT ZERO.
That would be me...
ARITY

Three more people had gone down the spew highway by then, and the whole plane smelled pretty much like you'd expect. I don't know if you've ever been in a giant sealed metal tube with a bunch of people losing their chicken-or-fish lunch, but let's just say the air wasn't so fresh anymore. Even the passengers who didn't know me were looking my way like I deserved to go to jail.

And the worst part was, everyone thought I'd done it on purpose. I heard a bunch of kids saying stuff like "Poor Bobby," and "What did Bobby ever do to Rafe?" Like *I* was the bully in this picture. *Me!*

Put it this way. If you're in a group with Miller the Killer, and everyone thinks *you're* the problem? You've had a bad day.

I apologized, and apologized, and apologized, but it didn't do any good. Bobby wouldn't talk to me, and Mrs. Stricker made me sit next to her the whole rest of the way.

She wasn't interested in my side of the story, either. She just wanted to make sure I learned some kind of lesson. And believe me,

Mrs. Stricker has a world-class history of doing exactly that.

Here, I'll show you. If you know my story, you might even remember some of this stuff.

EXHIBIT A

And then this:

And then this:

EXHIBIT C

So I didn't know *what* to expect from Mrs. Stricker this time. All I can tell you is that I never would have predicted it in a jillion years.

"Rafe," she said, "I've tried everything I can think of with you. So this time, we're going to do things a little differently."

Differently? I didn't like the sound of that.

"What do you mean?" I said.

"I've made a decision," she told me. "I'm putting you in charge. *You* are going to be the Editor in Chief for our Living-Learning Report in London," she said matter-of-factly.

"What?" I said. "Are you sure you don't have me confused with someone else?"

She didn't even crack a smile.

"Clearly," she said with a little shake of her head, "I can't motivate you to be a better citizen of our school, but perhaps your fellow students can."

"But nobody even likes me!" I kind of blurted out. It was embarrassing, but it was the truth. "How am I supposed to be *anything* in chief?"

"Great leaders don't focus on being liked," Mrs. Stricker told me. "They focus on leading. You should consider this an opportunity."

Yeah, sure, I thought. An opportunity to crash and burn faster than a hot-air balloon made out of Swiss cheese with ten anchors strapped to the basket.

"What about that contest? And those prizes?" I said.

"You'll be just one part of the team, which I will be supervising," Stricker said.

"But—," I said.

"Your other choice is to take an automatic F for the unit," she said. "I can't promise what that will do to your chances of finishing middle school on time, but that's up to you."

"Okay, okay, I'll do it," I said, because the only thing that sounded harder was spending a whole extra year at HVMS.

It was like the apocalypse, only worse.

Stricker had struck again.

WELCOME TO LONDON, LOSER

By the time we landed at Heathrow Airport in London, my brain was ready to explode. There was way too much to figure out now, and we hadn't even started yet.

For one thing, I really wanted *someone* to know that whole barf-fest on the plane wasn't on purpose. I tried talking to Ms. Donatello while we were at the baggage claim, but I didn't get very far with her, either. It went like this:

"Ms. Donatello, can I talk to you for a sec—"

"Not now, Rafe."

That was it. Then she went to gather some kids that wandered away from the group, and take another roll call, and get everyone moving toward the "motor coaches" outside. I thought I must have misheard Ms. Donatello, because I couldn't even imagine what she was talking about.

It turns out, that's just what they called these little buses we were taking to the hotel. *Motor coaches*. There were two of them, so I hung back while Miller, Bobby, and a bunch of people got on the first one. Then I just kept my head down, found a seat, and tried to act invisible.

I didn't even know I was sitting behind Jeanne and stupid perfect Jared until I heard Jeanne say something.

"Pretty rough flight, huh?" she said.

When I looked up, I could just see her through the

little crack between the headrests. I checked behind me just to be sure, but I was pretty sure she'd said it to me, and I'm not going to lie...I almost wanted to cry. At least *someone* was talking to me. And of course it was Jeanne, because she's awesome. She has friends like the Atlantic has water, but she's nice to everyone. And not fake nice, either.

"Yeah, pretty rough," I said.

Jeanne didn't say anything else. Jared was next to her, but he was busy talking to some other kids across the aisle. So after gathering a little bit of courage, I leaned forward and kept talking to Jeanne through that little crack.

"Hey, Jeanne? I just want you to know something. What happened up there wasn't on purpose, I swear. I was just trying to make Bobby laugh. And I know what you're probably thinking—it was still a stupid thing to do. I totally get that. I get why people are mad, and I'm going to make it up to them. I mean, to Bobby. Well, to everyone. Somehow.

"But I also wanted to say thanks for talking to me. I guess that sounds lame, huh? But I really kind of needed it. So, uh, just...thanks for listening, anyway."

Once I started, I didn't want to stop. I was going to tell her about the whole Editor in Chief disaster, too, so she wouldn't think I stole her job. But then Jared turned around again, and I sat back fast. The last thing I needed was for him to hear me blabbing my guts out like the Grade A doofus I was.

"Hey, Jeanne?" Jared said. *"Jeanne!"*

"Huh?" she said.

That's when Jeanne reached up, pulled back her hair, and took out one of her earbuds.

"What's up?" she said.

"Look!" Jared said. He was pointing out the window, and Big Ben was right there. You could also see the London Eye, all lit up at night, and a double-decker bus was just driving by. I guess we really were in London.

And I'd just given one of the biggest speeches of my life to the back of a bus seat. She must have popped them in while I was trying work up the guts to say something.

So even though I was there with a whole bunch of other kids, in the middle of a giant city stuffed with millions of people from around the world, I felt...lonely. If that makes any sense.

Really, really lonely.

WELCOME * H.V.M.S.

THE HELMSMAN'S ARMS

It was 10:45 p.m. London time when we got to the hotel. That's six hours later than it was at home. So basically, they wanted everyone to go to bed at quarter to five in the afternoon and not get up until morning.

Totally fine with me.

Our hotel was this big place called the Helmsman's Arms. It seemed like a creepy name to me. Maybe it was supposed to be *arms* like *weapons,* but I kept thinking about loose body parts.

I wasn't about to push my way to the

front of any lines, either. So I waited around while everyone else got their luggage and room numbers and stuff. When I finally made my way to one of the chaperones, Andrea Chin's dad, Mr. Chin was all set to help me. He seemed okay.

"Rafe, you're in Room 566," he said, and handed me a plastic card in a little envelope. "You can catch the elevator with that last group over there. Fifth floor, got it?"

"Got it," I said.

I could see a bunch of people waiting for the elevator, so I started walking that way. Then as soon as Mr. Chin wasn't looking anymore, I took a quick turn and hit the stairs instead. I didn't like the idea of squeezing into one little box with twelve people who hated me right now.

So I counted the flights instead, and walked up five levels. I just wanted to get to my room, apologize to Bobby for the hundred and sixteenth time, and get some shut-eye.

As soon as I came out of the stairwell and into the hall, Mrs. Stricker was standing there with another clipboard. She didn't exactly look happy to see me.

"What are you doing here? This is the girls' floor," she said. "Boys are on the fifth floor."

"But I thought—"

"You're already on thin ice with me, Mr. Khatchadorian. Do you really want to try my patience?"

"No," I said. "I just—"

"Go!" she said.

A bunch of girls were still out in the hall, and all of them were watching me now, like some little kid who had just wandered into the ladies' room. Like I needed anything *else* to be embarrassed about.

So I turned around and went back down the stairs to ask Mr. Chin if he'd made a mistake.

"Did you count the second floor as the first floor or the second floor?" he asked me.

I figured I was just tired, because that made no sense at all—right?

"Huh?" I said.

"In England, the first floor is known as the ground floor. That's where we are now. Then comes the first floor. And so on. It should be perfectly well marked in the elevator," he said, like there was probably something wrong with *me*.

"Uh…it is," I said. "Sorry about that. I've got it now."

By the time I got to the fifth floor (which was really the sixth floor), Mr. Rourke was waiting in the hall by himself.

"Did you get lost?" Mr. Rourke asked me.

"Kind of," I said.

"Well, it's past curfew," he said, and pointed down the hall.

When I finally got to Room 566, I put my card in the little slot, waited for the green light to come on, and then opened the door.

"What's up?" Tyler Fleischman said when I came in. He was sitting on one of the beds, channel-surfing. Bobby was on the other bed, playing some game.

"Uh—," I said.

"You're next door," Bobby said. "We switched."

"What do you mean?" I said.

"We already talked to Mrs. Stricker and she said it was okay. I'm going to room with Tyler now," he said.

Tyler held out a different key card. "This one's

yours, and you're supposed to give me that one," he told me.

What could I say? I know when I'm not wanted. (Believe me, I know! Lots of practice on that front.) Besides, if there was ever someone I owed, it was Bobby Flynn.

"Yeah, okay," I said. "I'll, uh....see you later, I guess—"

"Bye," Bobby said. He didn't even look at me.

So now I was in Room 568, which was one over. I walked next door, stuck my card in the slot, and...

Have you already figured out what's coming next? Because I hadn't. I was too busy thinking about how Bobby hated me, and what I was going to do about all that.

Which makes this next part more like one of those scenes in a horror movie where you want to yell at the dummy on the screen.

But it's always already too late. And this time, *I'm* the dummy on the screen.

The music gets all spooky. I stick my key in the slot. I pull open the door of that dark, creepy hotel room...*CREEEEAAAAKKK*...and I walk straight into the shadows to meet my fate.

568
Don't go in there!
NOO!!
Don't open that door!
Turn around, DUMMY!!

TERROR IN ROOM 568

Hello?" I say.

It's dark in here. Really dark. I try the light switch but nothing happens. It would probably make sense to go back outside and get some help. But this is a horror movie, remember? So I do the opposite of that, and I keep on going.

There must be a lamp in here somewhere, I think. I can still see a little bit of where I'm going, from the light in the hall. So I take another step inside. Then my foot squishes on the carpet. I look down. When I raise my shoe, a trail of dark slime sticks to it from the floor.

"What the…?" I say, just before—

SLAM!

The door whams shut behind me. Now it's

pitch-black, and my heart is picking up speed. I feel my way up the hall, trying not to panic.

Then I remember my phone. Good idea! I pull it out of my pocket and light up the screen. It's not much, but it's something. I shine it around, trying to see where I'm going.

SCREECH! HISSSSS!

The sound makes me jump about eight feet—before I realize it was just a cat down in the alley.

"Phew," I say. I even laugh a little, because I was getting so paranoid for a second there.

But there's nothing scary here. It's just me,

an ordinary hotel room, and some weird-smelling furniture. (That *is* the furniture I'm smelling, right?)

Finally, I spot a lamp by the bed. Just what I've been looking for. I breathe another sigh of relief as I walk over, reach for the switch, and—

I FEEL SOMETHING TOUCHING ME!

A hand shoots up from the bed. Cold, clammy fingers close around my wrist. I try to scream, but nothing comes out.

That's when I see the flesh-eater lying there, like a sack of invisible bones just waiting for his next meal.

"Touch that light switch and you die," he growls.

And in those last few seconds before he starts turning me into his own personal three-course meal, I remember something.

I remember that in horror movies, there are two kinds of people. There are the ones who walk into dark, creepy hotel rooms alone at night. And then there are the ones who have a chance of surviving to the end of the movie.

Guess which one I am?

CHAPTER 12

TERROR IN ROOM 568: PART 2

"Wh-wh-what did you say?" I asked.

"I said…touch that light switch and you die," Miller told me.

He was already in bed, with the covers pulled up and everything. That was pretty weird, I thought. And I only managed to think *that* because I'd already thought—

I took my hand off the lamp and stepped back—out of Miller's reach.

"You're sleeping in there," he said. Then he pointed at the bathroom door.

"Say what?" I said.

"You heard me."

My eyes were starting to adjust to the dark. I could see Miller had his stuff all over the second bed. I also noticed there weren't any blankets or pillows on that bed.

Now I was totally confused. First of all, I'd ended up with Miller the Killer as my roommate, which was insane. Second, I'd been alone with him for at least forty-five seconds, and I was still standing. And third—

"Do you really expect me to sleep in the bathroom?" I said.

"Do you really want to live?" he said.

"Listen, Miller. I'm sorry about what happened on the plane," I told him. "For real. I mean it—"

"One more word, and I'm coming over there to turn you inside out," he said.

I believed him, too, and not just because Miller was twice my size.

So I didn't have a choice.

I went in the bathroom, closed the door, turned on the light, and sat down to figure out what should happen next.

Then I got up again, *locked the door,* and sat back down.

Something told me I wasn't leaving that room anytime soon.

FRIEND-MERGENCY

I do some of my best thinking in bathrooms. In fact, it wasn't all bad, being stuck in there. That tub was plenty big, and it was better than trying to sleep three feet away from Miller. He even gave me two pillows, so that counted as a win.

But that just meant I was good for the next eight hours. I still had the rest of the trip to worry about. Miller may have been my newest problem, but he wasn't the *only* problem. I had thirty-four more of those to deal with, one for every kid on this trip. How was I supposed to do this Editor in Chief thing when all thirty-four of them hated me? (Except maybe Jeanne, but throw in Mrs. Stricker, and we're back up to thirty-four haters.)

This was like a friend emergency. Or a *friend-*

mergency. I've had a few of those before, but never so many at the same time.

And that's when I went for my backup.

A lot of you might already know Leo's story. He was my twin brother, but he died a long time ago, when we were little kids. After that, he was more like my imaginary friend, which I know is kind of weird. But so is sleeping in a bathtub in London.

I don't talk to Leo nearly as much as I used to.

He got me through a lot of rough times back in the day (all right, a year ago). Now, mostly I just put him into the comics I draw. Still, he's always there if I need something.

"'Ello, 'ello, 'ello!" Leo said as soon as I thought of him.

"Hang on. You're not going to speak in an English accent the whole time, are you?" I asked.

"Why not, guv'nah?" he said. "It's bloomin' England!"

"Well, for one thing, not everyone talks that way here," I said. "And for another—*hello?* I could use a little non-accented help. I'm three thousand miles from home, I've got the world's toughest school assignment, everyone's mad at me, and I have a psycho killer for a roommate."

"Is that all?" Leo said.

"Very funny," I said. "I'm trying to come up with a plan."

"What have we got so far?" he asked.

"Not much," I said. "But I was thinking about what Mom told me, how I should be more friendly to people."

"Seriously?" Leo said. "I'm already bored."

"I'm not trying to be exciting," I said. "I'm trying to make people like me."

"You want to get people to like you?" Leo said. "Start with Jeanne Galletta."

I almost laughed. It's like Leo has a mind of his own sometimes, and it's even crazier than mine.

"Who said anything about Jeanne?" I said. "She's the only one who's *not* part of my problem."

"Exactly," Leo said.

"Huh?"

"Tell Jeanne how you feel about her," Leo said. "Like once and for all. For real this time. This is me, remember? And we both know you've been in love with her since the first day of middle school."

"I don't want to talk about Jeanne, okay?" I said. "I want to talk about a plan."

"Hellooo?" Leo said. "Dude, that *is* the plan. Believe me, if you get Jeanne to like you, then you won't be worrying about what everyone else thinks. It'll be like taking care of thirty-four problems in one shot. That's what you call a *Master* Plan."

"Yeah, maybe," I said. "*If* it had any chance of working. Which it definitely doesn't."

Not to mention, telling perfect Jared McCall's girlfriend that I was in love with her seemed about as smart as running into a wolf's den dressed as a lamb chop.

"Besides," I said, "if something was going to happen with Jeanne, it would have already happened by now."

"Or, maybe you never went for it," Leo said. "You never *really* tried."

"Whatever. I'm not doing it," I said. And since I was the one walking around in the real world, I got to decide. So I picked up my sketchbook and started drawing instead.

"Okay, fine," Leo said. "You let me know when you're ready to do something a little more brave than making comics and being nice to everyone."

And then he was gone. Poof! Just like that.

See, Leo's all about danger, risk, and excitement. If it's not big and crazy, he's not interested. And telling Jeanne how I really felt about her was like the definition of *crazy*.

Still, that didn't mean Leo was wrong. If I could have actually gotten Jeanne to like me (like that), then everything else probably would have looked like small potatoes. Too bad Leo's "Master Plan" was also totally unrealistic, totally impossible, and totally not-going-to-happen.

And even worse—now that he'd brought it up, I couldn't stop thinking about it.

Thanks a lot, Leo.

Chapter 14:
LOOZER AND LEO in:
SMELL YOU LATER
I love England!
There's Big Ben!
Everything's so... English.
Say cheese!
CLICK!

What next?
Look! It's the Queen!
Cheerio, lads!
Hi, Your Majesty!
CLICK!

Wow! What can top that?
Well, actually...
Here comes Jeanne.
Now's your chance. Tell her how you really feel!
I can't talk to Jeanne!

Why not?
I don't know what to say. Besides, she doesn't even know I'm alive.
Do it!
hhhHi!
PFFRT!
?!

Uhh...
I hate England.
Well, she definitely knows you're alive now.

THE STRANGEST THING EVER

That bathtub was more comfortable than you'd think. I don't even know when I fell asleep, but I did—right until something woke me up in the middle of the night.

It took me a second to remember where I was, and why my bed felt so bathtubby. But then I heard that noise again.

Someone was crying.

It must have been some loud crying, too, because I could hear it all the way in that bathroom. Was it Bobby? Or Tyler? Or someone in the room on the other side?

I sat up and listened closer. There was this gulpy sound, and then one of those shaky breaths you only get when you cry.

And then I realized it wasn't that loud, after all. It was coming from closer than I'd thought. In fact, it was coming from the other side of that bathroom door.

Yeah, that's right. It was Miller.

Crying.

Miller was crying.

For real.

WHAT. THE. HECK?

I had so many questions, I felt like I was being attacked!

Once I was done dying of shock, I knew I had two choices. I could try to go back to sleep, or I could investigate a little further.

Well—DUH. This was *waaaay* too big to walk away from.

I got out of the tub and tiptoed over to the door. That's when I heard Miller talking, too. He was just whispering, and it sounded like he was on the phone with someone, but I couldn't hear any words.

So I put my hand on the doorknob and turned it about a hundredth of an inch, just to see if it made any noise.

It didn't. Then I turned it a little more. And a little more. It took forever, but I finally got the door open, just wide enough to stick one ear through.

"But I already told you—," Miller said.

Then there was a long silence, except for a couple of wet sniffs.

"I know," he said. "But I—"

Someone kept cutting him off. Was some girl breaking up with him over the phone? Was he homesick? Did his parole officer just call with bad news? This was Miller, after all. I was ready to believe anything.

I can't explain it, Mr. Miller, but it's your fists. They're shrinking. I've never seen anything like it.
I'm breaking up with you. You're just not mean enough!
Sorry, son. We're reducing your allowance to five hundred bucks a week.

But the real question was—what did I do with this now? Was I supposed to feel sorry for Miller? Because weirdly enough, part of me did.

Was I supposed to use it against him somehow? That's not really my style. But I wasn't about to ignore it, either. Not in a million years.

So by the time I was tiptoeing back to my tub/bed, I'd figured out a few things.

1. I was going to find out what was up with Miller, one way or another.

2. I couldn't let Miller know I'd heard him crying. If he knew I was listening in like that, he'd wipe me out completely, just to erase that piece of information from the planet.

3. My trip to London had just gotten a lot more complicated.

4. A lot more dangerous, too.

5. Somewhere in my crazy imagination, Leo the Silent was smiling.

CHAPTER 16

GOOOOOOD MORNING!

In the morning, Miller was back to his old self. I know because when I woke up, he was right there in my face, making sounds like a gorilla trying not to laugh.

"What are you doing?" I said, sitting up fast. I guess I forgot to relock that bathroom door in the middle of the night.

"Get out," he growled.

"Yeah, all right," I said, getting out of the tub. "But now that I spent a whole night in here, we're even for what happened on the plane. Okay?"

"We'll see," Miller said, and slammed the bathroom door closed behind me.

In other words, we weren't even yet.

In fact, by the time he came back out, he was

smiling bigger than ever. And when I went to brush my teeth, I found out why.

"What'd you do with my toothbrush?!" I yelled. And I heard some more of that gorilla giggling from the other room.

"Nothing," Miller said. "I mean…I might have cleaned my toenails a little bit—"

"WHAT?" I said.

"Don't be a baby," Miller said.

Oh man. This was EXACTLY what I thought rooming with Miller would be like. In the worst possible way.

"So NOW we're even," I said. "Okay?"

"Sure," Miller said. "Whatever."

And that's when I saw my best pen sitting on the bathroom floor with the cap off. Which is also just before I looked in the mirror, and found out what all that stupid gorilla giggling was *really* about when I woke up.

So despite whatever had been bothering Miller in the middle of the night, he was in a way better mood now. Probably because the sun was up and he could get back to playing with his own personal stress ball.

Also known as *me*.

CHIEFLY SPEAKING

Speaking of stress, things only got weirder at breakfast. That's when Mrs. Stricker got up to make the morning announcements.

Well—*announcement,* I guess. Singular. It might've just been one, but it was a doozy.

"I hope you all have your cameras and travel journals with you this morning," she said. "I expect you all to take good notes as we set out today. And on that topic, I'd like to announce that the Editor in Chief for our Living-Learning Report will be..."

There was only about a nanosecond between that part of Mrs. Stricker's sentence and the next part, but I swear, it was enough time for every eyeball in the room to turn Jeanne's way.

Right before Stricker said—

"...Rafe Khatchadorian."

And—*PINNNGGGG!!!!*

That's the sound of the giant pin you could hear dropping in the room after Mrs. Stricker said I'd be in charge. It was *that* quiet. I think everyone thought they must have heard wrong, like maybe Mrs. Stricker had given the job to some new kid named *Schmafe Schmatchadorian*.

Because the real truth was even weirder than that.

The first one to speak up was Simon.

"Really?" he said.

The second, third, and fourth ones were Katrina, Maya P., and Lily. I mean, if laughing counts.

"Yes, really," Mrs. Stricker said.

Then she named off the topic leaders—Isaiah for arts, Alison for politics, Mackenzie for history, Simon for science, and...of course...Jeanne for current events.

Because, you know, things weren't already weird enough.

When I looked over at Jeanne, she looked like she was about to cry. She'd probably already been thinking about how that Editor in Chief job was going to look on her pre-pre-college applications. Is that a real thing? I don't even know. I just know that seeing Jeanne fight back those tears made me feel like the lowest piece of dirt on the dirt clod on the bottom of the shoe of a bottom-feeding bottom-feeder.

It didn't help that Jared was staring at me, too,

like I'd just stolen something from his girlfriend. Which I kind of had. Even if it wasn't on purpose. (Sound familiar? It should.)

In other words, Day Two was off to just as good a start as Day One.

GET ON THE BUS

When we came out of the hotel, there was this big double-decker tour bus waiting for us. It was all open on the top level like a giant convertible, so you *know* everyone went straight for those seats.

That left me two options. One—I could stay down below with Mrs. Stricker and the driver, like a gigantic loser. Or two—I could go up with everyone else, where they could all see me sitting by myself with nobody to talk to...also like a gigantic loser.

I figured I might as well be outside. At least then I'd get more of a view, more fresh air, and less Mrs. Stricker. I even snagged one of the good seats near the front—until I let Cedric and Olivia take it instead. I was still trying to do the whole *nice* thing, but they didn't even thank me.

Then, when Mrs. Stricker took roll call and got to my name, Miller just kept the yuks coming and answered for me. It was actually a half-decent imitation of my stupid, cracking voice—one-half "Here!" and one-half "HONK!"

But I wasn't laughing. Not like everyone else was.

The good news is, things got a little better after that. It turns out that London's a really cool city! Once we finally got rolling, we saw about eighteen different parks and this whole waterfront with all kinds of stuff to do along the River Thames (which sounds like *"Tems"* if you're speaking British, by the way. You'd think since they invented English over here, they'd be better at pronouncing it right). It seemed like every time I turned around, I was looking at either the world's oldest buildings or the newest skyscrapers on the planet. They have this one called the Gherkin that looks about one massive ignition away from liftoff.

At first, I tried taking notes for my report, but it wasn't so easy on a moving bus. I tried drawing, too, but it all came out looking like this:

Yeah, that wasn't going to win any contests! So I took out my phone and turned on the video instead.

That was the way to go. I got some great shots of the Victoria and Albert Museum, and this giant store called Harrods, and Buckingham Palace—which, to be honest, I thought was going to look like a big castle but doesn't.

And here's what I figured out pretty quick after that. When you've got no one to talk to, a video camera can be your best friend. Seriously. It totally gave me something to do besides sitting there feeling like I had a contagious disease.

That was when I started getting *really* into it,

too. I remember because when that bus turned into Green Park, I tried my first real movie move with the camera. I pointed my phone back at Buckingham Palace, then swooped it up toward the sky, turned around fast, and came down again, like we'd just landed in the park out of nowhere.

Then I played it back for myself, and I'm not going to lie—it looked awesome! It was like I'd strapped the camera to some superhero's head just before he made the world's biggest leap.

So I kept going.

I panned around the park, up into the trees, down again, and then way in close on some black swans in the water. The way they were flapping their beaks, it looked like you could give them human voices in the video and do something funny with that. Probably with an English accent.

I didn't know how all this was going to fit into our Living-Learning Report yet, but I didn't even care. I was finally having a good time.

In fact, I started thinking maybe this was my new thing. Maybe instead of drawing all the time, I'd make videos instead. Cool videos. The kind that go mega-viral in a matter of seconds.

And maybe...just maybe...after someone discovered me on YouTube, everything would take off. I'd be a real director then, working with big stars and making even bigger money. I'm talking about the kind of cash that buys you sharks that do tricks in your aquarium overlooking the Hollywood Hills, and private jets to Hawaii for breakfast, because sometimes you just *have* to have those pineapple pancakes at your favorite place—

"*What* is he doing?"

"I have no idea."

"He is so weird sometimes. It's like he lives in his own world or something."

"I know, right?"

Ooops. I was getting so into my video that I kind of forgot everyone else was there. It felt like the real world went away for a minute, and it was just me and my phone-camera, doing our thing.

That was, until I heard those girls behind me. That brought me right back to Planet Earth. I recognized Sabra's and Katrina's voices, but I didn't have the nerve to turn around.

"I mean, he's not so shrimpy anymore," Katrina said.

That was a good thing, right? They noticed I'd gotten taller. Maybe not tall. But tall*er*. At least I wasn't the shortest kid in the class anymore.

"And he's cuter than he was in sixth grade," Sabra said.

Me? Cuter? Really? I couldn't believe it.

"Ew! You think Rafe's cute?" Katrina said.

"I mean, just in a dorky kind of way," Sabra said.

"Well, I guess I can see that," Katrina said, right before they both cracked up.

And I thought, *Yeah, that's more like it.*

Welcome back to the real world.

TOWER POWER

Our first stop was the Tower of London. If you haven't heard of it, it's this thousand-year-old fort where a bunch of people got their heads chopped off back in the really, really old days.

So yeah, most of us were pretty interested.

Our tour guide was a guy named Gordon. He had this old-school uniform with a big hat and told us he was a "yeoman warder of the Tower." They nicknamed those guys Beefeaters, because supposedly back when it was a real prison, the guards were allowed to eat all the best meat from the king's fridge. I wanted to ask if you could be a vegetarian and still work there, but I decided to keep my mouth shut instead.

Today's Specials
Roast Beef
Chipped Beef
Beef
Beef Burgers
Beef on Beef
Leftover Beef
Actually, I'll just have a salad....

Anyway, Gordon was pretty cool. He was also way funnier than you think someone could be, talking about things like the Bloody Tower and Traitors' Gate and how they used a sword instead of an ax on Anne Boleyn's head. That special treatment was because she was King Henry VIII's wife, and also because "an ax can get a bit messy," according to Gordon.

"Some say London is the world's most haunted city," he told us, "and that this very tower is its most haunted building."

He winked when he said the last part, but it gave me the shivers. If Gordon was right, then all those executions happened right there, on the exact same ground where we were standing.

So, just to be on the extra-safe side, I kept my camera running. I'm not saying I believe in ghosts, but if they *were* real, and I got a picture of one, can you imagine how fast we'd win that contest?

So when Gordon said it was time to "queue up" (which means get in line) for the gems and jewels part of the tour, I was a little bummed. I wanted to stay outside and see more of the creepy, ghosty, prisony stuff. Visiting a bunch of jewelry in glass cases didn't sound nearly as cool to me.

And it wasn't. In fact, what happened next was extremely *not* cool.

And, of course, it was all my fault.

RULES AND JEWELS

The first thing we had to do before we went inside was hear about all the rules. They had more rules for seeing the Crown Jewels than Mrs. Stricker has for Hills Village Middle School.

Actually, no, they didn't. Nobody has more rules than Mrs. Stricker. But there were a lot, anyway.

"Please maintain an orderly line, keep your voices down, respect the boundaries, do not touch the cases, keep moving, do not block access for others…," Gordon recited, like he'd said it a hundred times before.

I didn't even catch all of it, but I got his drift. NO MESSING AROUND WITH THE JEWELS. And no video, either, so I had to put my camera away.

Gordon said there were more than twenty-three thousand diamonds, emeralds, rubies, and sapphires in the vault, guarded every hour of every day of the year. I asked him how much it was all worth, but he just said the collection was priceless, which is like saying it cost infinity, give or take a couple of dollars.

For me, the coolest part was the entrance. You walk in through these giant four-ton doors, like walking into a real bank vault.

And then there were the people movers. Once we got inside, the way to see everything was to stand on these conveyor belts, like the electric sidewalks at the airport. Then you just kind of ride past the jewels without having to walk or anything.

I'll be honest. I thought it was kind of boring, like taking an hour to walk through a jewelry store. Ghosts and rolling heads beat diamonds and rubies, every time. Especially if they're not even giving out free samples.

But then I noticed Bobby. He had his notebook out and kept trying to get to the front where he could see better. I guess he wanted to write about those jewels for his part of the report.

I didn't mention this before, but Bobby's one of the shortest kids in our class. Just like I used to be, which was just the worst. So I took a step back and made some room for him on the conveyor belt.

"Go ahead," I said.

I didn't want Bobby to think I was trying *too* hard to make friends, but I still wanted to do something nice for him. Especially something that had zero chance of making him throw up.

Bobby didn't say anything. He just moved around to get a better view, while I got out of his way.

For about half a second.

It's pretty dark in that vault, so I didn't see exactly what happened. All I know is that when I stepped out of Bobby's way, someone else's foot got tangled up with mine. And the last thing I saw before everything went kerflooey was Jared McCall looking down at me…smiling.

The next thing I knew, I spun around and fell right into one of those big jewelry cases—right before I ricocheted off it and hit the floor. All I left behind was a noseprint and two streaks where my hands slid down the glass.

That conveyor belt was still going, too. A second later, I got spat out onto the carpet while a bunch of people jumped out of the way, trying not to get knocked over like bowling pins.

Three words: Major. Security. Disaster.

A bunch of guards came running over, along with Mrs. Stricker. All the lights clicked on. Everyone stopped what they were doing. And I was wondering how this could have gone so bad, so fast. *AGAIN*.

"Do NOT touch the glass!"

"No horseplay will be tolerated in here!"

"Young man, get off the ground!"

"What is going on here?" Mrs. Stricker yelled.

"Rafe tried to push Bobby," someone said.

Wha? I looked over, and it was Jared's best friend, Colin, who'd said it. Jared was just standing there, staring at me. And he was *still* smiling.

But then Bobby spoke up next.

"It wasn't Rafe's fault," Bobby said.

And I was like—*huh???*

"He was just trying to get out of my way," he said. "That's all. It was an accident."

I guess Bobby knew I was trying to do him a favor. And maybe he'd even started to figure out that I was never trying to make him spew on that plane in the first place.

So even though all those guards were looking for someone to blame, and Jared had *probably* just tripped me on purpose (even though I couldn't prove it), and I still had Mrs. Stricker hating me, it was also kind of cool, too. Like maybe, finally, being nice had started to pay off, just a tiny bit.

With Bobby, I mean. I still had everyone else to deal with.

Starting with Mrs. Stricker.

THIN ICE

When everyone went outside to get fish and chips for lunch, Mrs. Stricker made me stay back for another talking-to.

"Mrs. Stricker," I told her, "I know how that looked, but it's like Bobby said—"

"What I know, Rafe, is that trouble seems to follow you wherever you go," she said. "Whether it's your fault or not."

"But—," I said.

"I don't want to hear about your *but,*" she told me. "Do you understand? Not one more *but* out of you. As far as I'm concerned, that was your last *but.*"

I honestly didn't mean to laugh, but come on! You would have, too, right? You can only listen to a grown-up say *butt* so many times in a row without busting up.

"Is something funny?" Mrs. Stricker barked.

"No!" I said, and then I tried to think about the saddest things I could, to keep from cracking another smile while Mrs. Stricker finished yelling at me.

The good news was, I didn't get in any more trouble. Mrs. Stricker didn't cut off my head or put me in a time-out or whatever you do for detention when the detention room is on the other side of the ocean.

The bad news was, she told me I was "back on thin ice." If I didn't "watch myself" and "fly right" for the rest of the trip, I was headed straight for that automatic F. Which meant staying in middle school another whole year.

In other words, the pressure was still on. More than ever. I needed to figure out this Editor in Chief business, ASAP (that's how editors say "as soon as possible"). And there was only one person I could think of who might help me with it.

The trick was going to be getting her to talk to me.

December
Christmas Canceled!
Homework...
LOST DOG
Have You Seen Junior
Asparagus "Surprise"

A LITTLE HELP? ANYONE?

Once Mrs. Stricker let me go, I went outside, where everyone was having lunch by the river. I skipped the fish and chips and went looking for Jeanne instead.

When I found her, she was eating with Morgan and Alison, which didn't help. The two of them looked like they wanted to strap some chum to my arms, throw me in the river, and hope some sort of river shark came swimming along.

At least Jared wasn't there, because I had enough on my mind already. Most of all right now, I had to worry about Jeanne.

"Hey, Jeanne, can I talk to you?" I said. "Like, maybe in private?" Except, of course, it came out like this:

I think my voice hates me. Either that or I have the worst luck in the history of hormones.

Jeanne didn't laugh, though, unlike her friends. Which was nice. I couldn't tell what she was thinking, but she did get up and follow me away from Morgan and Alison, so I could finish embarrassing myself in private.

"What's up?" she asked me.

I tried to swallow, but my throat was like one big piece of dried leather.

Now that we were alone, I couldn't stop thinking about what Leo had told me the night before. It was like he was right there, coming in loud and clear.

Finally, I got it out.

"The truth is, I need to ask you a favor," I told her. "But I also want to say that I'm really sorry about the whole Editor in Chief thing. I never asked for that job. I swear."

"It's okay, Rafe," Jeanne said. "I know."

"You do?"

"Yeah," she said. "I mean, come on. This is me you're talking to. We're not exactly strangers."

I wasn't really sure what that meant. I mean, I understood the words, but I didn't know what Jeanne was trying to *say*.

"You seemed kind of upset about it this morning," I said.

"I was," Jeanne said. "But I think I was mostly embarrassed."

"Why should you be embarrassed?" I asked. "You didn't do anything."

"I know," she said. "It's just that I'm used to being in charge with that kind of stuff. And now... well...*you're* in charge."

"Ohhh," I said. I was starting to figure it out. "So, are you saying you were embarrassed because you didn't get to be Editor? Or because *I* did?"

"Neither," Jeanne said. "I don't mean it like that. It's just...I really wanted us to win that contest," Jeanne said.

I'm not going to lie. That hurt my feelings. A lot.

Which is stupid. I mean, it's not like I thought I could do a better job than Jeanne. I didn't think I could do it *at all*. So why should it matter if Jeanne thought so too?

But here's the thing. It did matter.

"This is coming out all wrong," Jeanne said. "Please don't be mad, Rafe."

"I'm not," I said.

"Yes you are," she said.

Yes. I was. Sure, she was right about us probably losing the contest because of me, but it was super-confusing, too. I mean, trying to be mad at Jeanne is like trying to be mad at chocolate cake. How are you supposed to do that?

Meanwhile, my heart was pumping, my face was hot, and I felt like I'd just run a mile in concrete socks.

"I've got to go," I said.

"Rafe, come back!" Jeanne said. "Didn't you say you wanted to ask me a favor?"

But it was too late. I couldn't stop walking away now. So I just kept going—as far away from Jeanne as I could get.

And that many steps closer to that automatic F.

HISTORY AND MYSTERY

After dinner that night, I spent a long time in the Learning Center at the hotel. That was like a classroom they had set up for us, with tables and computers and stuff.

First, we had a team meeting. That's what Mrs. Stricker called it. All the topic leaders were there, including Jeanne, of course. Also Ms. Donatello, Mr. Rourke, Mrs. Stricker, and me.

And yeah, the whole thing was about as comfortable as a sandpaper straitjacket. Jeanne kept looking at me across the table, and I spent most of the time saying stuff like "Uh-huh," and "Okay," and "That sounds good," because everyone had better ideas than me.

When Mrs. Stricker asked what I thought the theme for our report should be, I said, "Um... London?"

People actually thought it was a joke. But the truth is, that's the best I could come up with on the spot. Everyone kept looking at me like they were wondering what I was doing there, and the whole idea of winning that contest was feeling more and more like climbing Mount Everest blindfolded during a snowstorm.

After I finished coming up with exactly *zero* good ideas for our theme, Mrs. Stricker said we should organize what we had so far by topic and start posting it online. But then I said I'd do that part myself.

And that was for two reasons.

Actually, three.

Well, actually, four.

1. I wanted out of that meeting the way a turkey wants out of a turkey sandwich.

2. I wasn't exactly in a hurry to go hang out in my room with Miller, either.

3. I was still trying to do at least one nice thing for everyone on the trip.

4. So far, I'd been nothing but deadweight. I

needed to show Mrs. Stricker I could do this. Even if I was pretty sure I couldn't.

Then, when everyone got up to leave, Jeanne kind of hung back a bit. She looked like she wanted to say something to me, and I think she was about to. But then Jared showed up out of nowhere.

I couldn't even look at Jared. I still didn't know for sure that he was the one who tripped me at the jewel display—but I was *pretty* sure. And the embarrassing truth is, I was kind of scared of him. He wasn't as big and strong as Miller, but he was still bigger and stronger than me, and way more popular, too. And in my world, that's like having a whole extra set of fists.

I didn't know what to say to Jeanne anyway. I kind of owed her an apology, but at the same time, she really owed me one, too. Not that it mattered, because a second later, she and Jared went off to do whatever it is popular people do with their friends in London. And I was left in the Learning Center, by myself.

Maybe Day Three would be better than Day Two, I thought. But what I didn't know was that Day Two hadn't ended yet. In fact, it was about to get a whole lot more interesting.

SNOOP ON THE LOOSE

It was just before curfew when I finished working in the Learning Center and headed upstairs. I pretty much expected some kind of Miller-related disaster to be waiting up there for me. Like maybe all my boxers would be flushed down the toilet. Or worse.

But when I opened the door, Miller was just sitting on his bed and talking on the phone. The second he saw me, he told whoever it was that he had to go. Then he jumped up and headed straight for the bathroom door.

"I'm taking a shower," he said. "You wait out here."

As if I was going to follow him in there?

Two seconds later, he was in there with the

water running, and I was wondering what had just happened. It didn't seem like he was crying or anything, but something was definitely up.

It seemed like a perfect chance to do a little looking around and see what I could find out. If this were my sister, I'd call it "snooping." But this was me, so let's call it…"investigative reporting."

And there was plenty to investigate. The room looked like Hurricane Miller had just hit, right on top of Tornado Miller, and just after Earthquake Miller. Seriously, Miller was a bigger slob than me, and that's saying something.

The first thing I saw was Miller's report packet. It was sitting half under the bed and looked like he hadn't even brought it with him that day. I don't think he was too worried about getting a good grade. Or any grade, really. I think Miller had something else on his mind—but what was it?

Mostly, I was interested in his phone. It was just sitting where he'd tossed it on the nightstand, partly hidden by a hotel brochure, three empty water bottles, and about eighteen different candy wrappers.

I really wanted to see who Miller had been

talking to when he was crying the night before. But I didn't want to actually touch his stuff. That just felt a little gross. I mean, even Miller deserved his privacy.

Besides, when my finger maybe, kind of, accidentally brushed against the phone to turn it on, a security screen lit up. I'd have to figure out some other way to find out what was going on with him.

"WHAT ARE YOU DOING?" Miller roared behind me.

When I turned around, he was standing there in all his clothes, with his head soaking wet. He had a towel in his hand, but mostly he was dripping all over the floor.

"*That* was your shower?" I said. "You must be going for a world record—"

Miller took a step closer.

"I said, what are you *doing?*"

"Nothing," I said. By now, I was practically passing out and peeing my pants at the same time. It felt like I was standing under a heat lamp, and all I wanted to do was change the subject.

"I was just, um…," I said.

"Just *what?*" he said.

When I looked down at his phone again, I saw that hotel brochure, and picked it up.

"I was just looking at this," I said.

"What for?" Miller said. He was squinting at me now, like he wasn't done being suspicious yet (which made sense—I don't think I was selling this very well). It also meant I wasn't done being maybe-dead yet.

I looked at the brochure again. On the cover, it said, "Welcome to the Helmsman's Arms!" and "Complimentary Wi-Fi!" and "Enjoy our seasonal roof terrace."

And I thought, *Bingo!*

"I was thinking about checking out the roof of this place," I said. "You want to come?"

I don't think he was expecting that. Heck, I was barely expecting it myself until it popped out of my mouth. But the faster I got Miller away from the scene of my not-quite-a-crime, the better.

"Huh. What about the security guy?" Miller said.

"There's ways around that," I told him. Which was true.

Mrs. Stricker had hired this overnight guard to make sure we all stayed in our rooms while the chaperones were asleep. He had a little desk in the hall, but mostly he kept on the move, from the boys' floor, to the girls' floor, to the boys' floor, to the girls' floor, just all night. But that also meant he was only around half the time.

"Yeah, okay," Miller said. "I'm in."

Which is right around when I started thinking my great idea wasn't so great after all. I mean, a high rooftop isn't exactly the safest place in the world to hang out with someone who has the word *Killer* in his name. All kinds of stuff could happen up there—most of it bad.

"You know what?" I said. "Maybe we should just watch a movie or something instead. That could be just as—"

"Too late," Miller said. He was already heading for the door and dragging me there with him. "Because now you've got me interested, and you're the one who knows how to do it. Let's go."

So, we went.

WHAT COULD POSSIBLY GO WRONG?
Let me back in!!!
AAAAAAAA
Don't. Touch. My. Stuff!
ok!

MISSION: ROOF-POSSIBLE

Before we went anywhere, I looked at the hotel map on the back of our door. It showed where the stairwell was, in case we needed to get out in an emergency.

But we didn't need to go down right now. We needed to go up.

The good news was, every time the security guy opened that stairwell door to head down to the girls' floor, it made this squeaking sound and then slammed shut behind him when it closed. So we could hear when he was on the move, no problem.

The bad news was, we had to use that same door to get to the roof. It was going to be risky, but not impossible.

As soon as we heard the next *squeeeeeeeeeak*

and *SLAM!*, I opened our hotel room door and leaned out into the hall.

"Anyone?" Miller whispered behind me.

"Nope."

It was deserted. But there was one more piece of bad news. When I looked down, I saw a piece of blue tape stuck to the edge of our door. It was the same on Martin and Kadir's door across the hall, and Rudy and Simon's door next to that. The difference was, those pieces of tape were still plastered across the crack like they were supposed to be.

I guess Security Guy had a few tricks up his sleeve. That tape was like an alarm system—if it was unstuck when he came back, that meant someone was out of their room.

"What do we do about that?" Miller said.

"We'll figure it out later," I whispered.

The damage was already done. It wasn't like we could put that tape back from *inside* our room, and they'd know if we just stayed out all night. So I closed the door behind us, pressed it into place to make it look like we were still there, and kept moving.

"Let's go," I told Miller.

We rushed on our tiptoes down to the stairwell door. Then I held up a hand for him to wait again. This was the trickiest part, and I wanted to go first.

The trick is to open a squeaky door at just the right speed. That way, if it creaks, it only makes a tiny sound. Then you kind of press through sideways so you don't open the door any more than you have to. I showed Miller and then he did it behind me.

The whole hotel was twelve stories high, so we huffed up a ton of stairs after that, until we got to a dead end at the roof door. A bunch of folding chairs were leaning against the wall on the landing, and I grabbed one. Miller opened the door, I propped it open, and we ducked outside.

It was dark on the roof. It looked like they had a restaurant up here when the weather was warmer. Now it was like a ghost restaurant, but that wasn't the cool part.

Spread out all around us, in every direction, there were city lights as far as I could see. We weren't *that* high up, but the view was awesome.

I took out my phone and started panning it back and forth for some good shots of the city.

"What are you doing?" Miller said.

"Making a movie," I said.

"Seriously?" he said.

"Well, a video, anyway. I'm still figuring it out," I told him.

"What a geek." He laughed.

Then we just hung out there for a while, not saying anything at all. It was actually, almost, kind of...peaceful. Which was pretty weird, with Miller standing right next to me.

And that's when I started thinking about something else.

I don't know why I didn't think of it before, but there was a reason Miller and I were stuck rooming together, and it wasn't just because Bobby kicked me out.

The thing was, neither one of us had any friends on this trip. All the Neanderthals Miller usually hung out with were back in Hills Village. Nobody wanted to room with him here, the same way nobody wanted to room with me. It was like the first thing we'd ever had in common.

Which I guess is how I ended up three thousand miles from home, hanging out on a dark rooftop with my biggest enemy ever, way past curfew.

Sometimes my life is so weird, I can't even believe it.

CHAPTER 26

CUTTING IT CLOSE

By the time we snuck back down to the fifth-floor hall, I still hadn't figured out what to do about that blue tape on our door.

But Miller was way into it now and getting in on the planning.

"Hey, I know!" he whispered. "What if we go through Bobby and Tyler's room? Then we can go out their window, around the outside, and back into *our* room."

"Seriously?" I said. "You must watch even more movies than me. And besides, that wouldn't help."

"Why not?" he said.

"Think about it," I said.

"*You* think about it," he snarled.

I was going to explain all the thousands of reasons that was a terrible idea, but then we heard a squeak and a slam coming from one floor down. That meant Security Guy was on his way back. Our time was up.

"What do we do now?" Miller said.

"Just…go in," I mumbled.

I was getting an idea. Maybe it would work, and maybe not. But at that point it wasn't like we could stay in the hall and blend into the wallpaper.

As soon as Miller got the door open, I booked it straight into the bathroom. I grabbed my pajama top out of my suitcase, put it on over my T-shirt, messed up my hair, and zoomed back over to the door.

"What are you doing?" Miller said, but I didn't stop.

"Just stay out of sight," I said. Then I opened the door again and leaned out into the hall, but only halfway so my pants and sneakers didn't show.

Security Guy spotted me right away. "You're supposed to be in your room!" he said, kind of shouting and whispering at the same time.

"Sorry," I said. I made my face all squinty like I'd just woken up and the bright lights were messing with my eyes. "I thought I heard someone out here."

"Ye-eaah," the guy said, like I was the dumbest kid who ever visited from America. "That was me."

"Oh," I said. "Right. Well...good night, then."

That was it. A second later, I was back inside with Miller breathing down my neck.

"What's that supposed to do?" he said.

I just put a finger up on my mouth to keep him quiet. A second later, I heard someone outside the door. Security Guy was right there.

Miller leaned in. So did I.

The next thing we heard was this tiny rubbing sound, while he put that piece of blue tape back in place. And…bam! Mission accomplished!

You should have seen the look on Miller's face. It was like he couldn't believe Rafe "Squeakadorian" had just pulled that off.

"Okay, that was actually kind of cool," he said.

"Thanks," I said.

It was like the best conversation we'd ever had. So I kept going.

"Hey, Miller?" I said. "Speaking of cool, it's kind of cold in that bathroom. I was just wondering if—"

"Nah. You're still sleeping in there," he said, and flopped out on his bed. "And keep it down, by the way. I'm beat."

Oh, well. It was worth a shot, anyway.

Chapter 27: Loozer and Leo in: How to Speak British

I guess we'll start without him. Can I get a volunteer from the audience?
I'll help.
!
Welcome to How to Speak British...

Lesson 1: If someone in England asks if you want some CHIPS, the answer is always yes.
French fries are called chips here. And chips are called crisps.
French Fries
CHIPS
And by the way, pudding doesn't come in cups over here.
French Fries
CHIPS

PUDDING
Sticky toffee sauce
But it's still REALLY good!
A truck is called a LORRY....
The elevator is a LIFT.
DING!
Soccer is called FOOT
BALL here. And footbal
is called AMERICAN
FOOTBALL.

In England, the bathroom is called the **LOO.**

LOO

LOO

EEEK!!

LOO NEWS

COOKIES ARE BISCUI

Z

"Z" IS CALLED ZED

There you are!

Sorry!

LOO

CLASS DISMISSED!!

UP AND AT ’EM

I woke up early the next morning. And I woke up thinking about all the work I had to do.

And Jeanne.

And Mrs. Stricker.

And the whole Editor in Chief thing.

Especially the Editor in Chief thing. I had three days left to get this report—and my act—together. So even though it was super-early, I got up and went down to the Learning Center. I was hoping maybe I could get a jump start on my day.

But you know who else gets up early to do homework? Smart people. People like Jeanne Galletta, for instance.

People *exactly* like Jeanne Galletta.

When I walked into that room, there she was,

working away at one of the computers.

Time-out for a second. You know those corny romantic comedies? Well, if life were *really* like those movies, I would have taken one look at Jeanne and said…

And Jeanne would say…

And I'd say...

And she'd hold up two tickets and say...

Then somehow, we'd end up outside in the pouring rain, where we'd probably kiss. No—definitely kiss. Just as a super-romantic pop hit starts playing in the background. That's what always happens in those movies, even though I'm not sure why pouring rain is supposed to be so romantic.

But it doesn't matter anyway, because we weren't in a movie, I don't look anything like that, and it wasn't even raining out. It was just me, standing there at six in the morning, looking like a doof.

"Hey," Jeanne said when she saw me.

"Hey," I said. "What are you doing down here?"

"I wanted to work on my report," she said. "What about you?"

"I wanted to work on *my* report," I said, and then we both kind of smiled. I probably should have said more, but my brain felt like the world's emptiest rubbish bin (that's what they call a garbage can in England).

So Jeanne went next.

"Rafe? I'm really sorry about yesterday," she said. "I do want to win that contest, but I shouldn't have said what I did."

"It's okay," I said. It was, too. "The truth is, you were right. I don't know what I'm doing, and I could really use some help."

Then Jeanne pulled out the chair next to hers and waved at me to come sit down.

"Maybe we could just start over," she said.

So even though it wasn't a movie, Jeanne almost made it feel like one. Which only made me like her more. Which was a good feeling and a bad feeling at the same time, if you know what I mean.

And if you don't, just trust me on this one.

ARTIST IN CHIEF

The time flew by after that, right up until breakfast. Jeanne showed me a bunch of great stuff we could do to make the report better, and I showed her some of my videos to see what she thought.

"These are great," she said—more than once. "They're like moving paintings. We should call you the *Artist* in Chief."

I liked that. A lot. Because the fact is, I have a way better chance of getting an A in art than I do in social studies (or anything else).

"Thanks," I said. "But I still don't know what I'm doing. I wish I was half as smart as you about all this stuff."

That's when Jeanne got this look on her face that I'd never seen before.

"Are you thinking what I'm thinking?" she asked me.

"I have no idea," I said. I never know what girls are thinking.

"Well, it's not *exactly* against the rules for me to help. And maybe we just don't tell Mrs. Stricker about it," Jeanne said. "So what do you think, Rafe? Do you want a secret partner?"

I actually wondered if she was joking. Jeanne's pretty straitlaced, if you know what I mean. She's not the first person you'd run to if you wanted to rob a bank. Or even fake a hall pass.

But it was also kind of perfect. Jeanne had the brains. I had the creativity. Jeanne was super-competitive. I knew a thing or two about being sneaky. Jeanne really wanted to win that contest. I really wanted whatever Jeanne wanted.

"Deal?" she said.

"*Secret* deal," I said, and we shook on it.

"What secret deal?" someone said.

When I turned around, Jared was standing in the Learning Center door. He'd just snuck right up on us, like the flu. (You know, if the flu played guitar and lacrosse, and had perfect teeth.)

“Hey, Jared!” Jeanne said. “I’m helping Rafe out with the Editor in Chief stuff, but we don’t want Mrs. Stricker to know. At least, not until we win that contest. Right, Rafe?”

“Uh…sure,” I said.

Supposedly, this was a good thing. Even Jared could see that, right? I hadn’t stolen Jeanne’s job, and everything she’d just told him proved it.

Right?

Still, there was something about the way Jared kept looking at me. I’m not going to say he seemed jealous, because, let's be honest—that would be like a turkey club being jealous of the dribble of mayo on the side of the plate.

But I don't think he liked me having secret meetings with his girlfriend. Or holding her hand, either. Which I wasn't doing, even if it looked that way. We were just shaking on it.

"So don't tell anyone about this, okay?" Jeanne asked him.

Jared gave that weird smile of his again, the kind that looked like the *opposite* of a smile.

"Sure," he said. "No problem."

Except it didn't sound like "no problem" to me at all.

It sounded a lot more like—*BIG problem.*

BEANS FOR BREAKFAST

Sorry, really quick time-out. Nothing to do with the story or all the disasters I had going on, but if you ever want a great breakfast, go to England! Baked beans with your eggs? *Delicious* (no matter how weird it sounds). Those Brits know how to start the day right.

Just saying—you won't go home hungry.

Again, sorry for the interruption. This breakfast just really deserved its own chapter—it was *that* good.

And now I'm hungry again.

CHAPTER 31

UNASSIGNED SEATS

By the time we got on the bus that morning, I was ready for Mrs. Stricker.

"You did this?" she asked me.

I'd just handed her a whole sheet of assignments for the day, so everyone would know who was supposed to write about what, who was taking pictures, and that kind of thing. It was all Jeanne's idea, but I wrote it up, so *technically,* I did do it.

"Well, this looks acceptable," Stricker said. "But we're going to need forty copies, one for each—"

"Right here," I said, and handed them over, still warm from the hotel copier.

"Oh," Stricker said. I don't think she saw that coming. (Thanks again, Jeanne!)

TUESDAY Assignments

ACTIVITY:	WRITTEN MODULES:	PHOTOGRAPHY:
Saatchi Gallery	Molly, Bobby, Mackenzie, Sabra	Kadir, Olivia, Simon
Old GLOBE Theatre	Rafe, Phinn, Katrina, Seth	Maya, Dominic, Emma G.
SOUTH BANK	Zoe, Jeanne, Colin, Emma W.	Tyler, Alison, Martin
LONDON EYE	Jared, Rudy, Andrea, Lily	Dryden, Robin, Makayla
Piccadilly CIRCUS	Isaiah, Morgan, Cedric	Hailey, Charlie, Katie, Shelby

Anyway, the only empty seat on the bus by then was next to Miller. I wasn't sure what to expect from him after our little roof mission, but he didn't say a word when I sat down. He didn't even look up from his phone. Not until Mrs. Stricker got to my name during roll call.

And then, sure enough—

I'll give him this much. His stupid imitation of me was getting better all the time. Mrs. Stricker just made another check mark and kept going.

Then—*PING!*—Miller got a new text and went right back to his phone. It was pretty clear something was still up with him. He was thumbing at that screen like he wanted to break through the glass.

Obviously that only made me *more* curious, but I had to be strategic about this. If I was patient, maybe I could find out what Miller's problem was *and* stop being his favorite chew toy for a while.

Emphasis on the *maybe.*

So I went back to scribbling in my notebook. I'd worry about Miller later. I had a ton of new ideas for videos, and I was getting pretty excited about this project, too. It was like a whole new ball game, now that I had a secret partner and an official new job title.

Or at least, an unofficial one. All thanks to you-know-who.

NOT BAD, JUST WEIRD

When we got to the Saatchi Gallery…well, first of all—*whoa!* I bet Ms. Donatello put that place on the schedule, because she likes weird art the way my dog likes sniffing butts (that's *a lot,* if you've never met Junior).

And this place was definitely weird with a capital *W*. I'd never seen art like it.

In one room, it was all just giant sculptures of nuts and bolts.

In another room, the walls and ceiling were covered in clear boxes filled with dirt and rocks, so it felt like you were underground.

Another room had a sound exhibit, where you were supposed to just sit on a bench and listen. There were recordings of waterfalls and leaky faucets, but also people talking about money at the same time.

So like I said—weird, weirder, and weirdest.

But also very cool. I kept my camera going the whole time. And best of all, Jeanne was right there to help out.

There was also a room with an exhibit called "Modern Nudes," but Mrs. Stricker put the lid on that one faster than a box of hornets. Nobody was allowed anywhere near it.

Meanwhile, everyone else was following their assignment sheets. They were taking pictures and making notes and doing everything like they were supposed to. It was amazing how much better the whole thing went, just from that simple plan Jeanne made up.

And as far as I could tell, Mrs. Stricker didn't suspect a thing. Or maybe she was too busy policing the naked stuff. Either way, that thin ice I'd been on was starting to feel just a little bit thicker.

So far, so good.

CHAPTER 33

THE WORLD'S A STAGE

You're probably going to think this is a strange question, but do you believe in signs?

I don't mean like STOP and NO TRESPASSING. I mean like when you think someone, somewhere, is trying to tell you something. Because that's what happened at our next stop, the Old Globe Theatre.

This place is super-famous. The original Globe was where William Shakespeare put on his own plays, back in the 1600s, and they still do his stuff there today.

So after we got a tour, they brought these actors out onstage to perform some scenes for us. The first one was from a play called *The Comedy of Errors*. After that, they did something from *Hamlet*.

Then finally, there was a scene from *Romeo and Juliet*. That was the one Shakespeare play I knew anything about, because Ms. Donatello made us read parts of it in sixth grade.

And here's where it really got interesting (at least in my head).

First of all, this was the part I'd assigned myself to do a written report on. I was taking notes instead of video this time and writing stuff down as fast as I could. So instead of writing "Romeo and Juliet" on the page, I just wrote "R+J."

That's right. R and J. Did you notice anything crazy awesome there? Like how those initials could stand for some other people?

Like maybe...Rafe and Jeanne?

I definitely noticed. Ms. Donatello says that Shakespeare's stuff is full of symbolism. So that got me thinking. Maybe this was a symbol for something.

Or a *sign*.

Like maybe Leo was right. Maybe I really was supposed to tell Jeanne how I felt about her. I mean, this was *Romeo and Juliet,* supposedly the greatest love story ever written.

Not only that, but the whole scene was about Juliet up on her balcony, saying, "Romeo, Romeo, wherefore art thou Romeo?" while he's down below, getting up the guts to talk to her.

Sound familiar?

I mean, don't get me wrong. Honestly, I probably knew it was just a big fat coincidence. But for a second there—a microsecond—it felt like *more* than a coincidence.

So by the time the scene was over, I decided that Leo was right. I had to say *something,* even if it was just one tiny little thing. Maybe I'd just mention that "R+J" part, and see what Jeanne said.

I could at least do that, right?

So after the show, when Jared was talking to someone else, I just *happened* to wind up standing next to Jeanne. Then I just *happened* to wait around until she noticed me.

"Did you like that?" I asked her.

"Yeah, it was great," Jeanne said.

"Especially the Romeo and Juliet stuff," I said. Then I kept going before my heart could start beating loud enough for Jeanne to hear it. "In fact, it was kind of funny, because—"

"Funny?" Jeanne gave me this *look*. "Did you ever read the whole play?" she asked.

"Just the parts Ms. D assigned," I said. "Why?"

"Well, spoiler alert, but—they both die at the end," she said.

"They do?" I said.

"Yep," Jeanne said. "It's one of Shakespeare's greatest tragedies."

She could say that again.

"Anyway, you were about to say something was funny?" she asked.

"Oh, uh...," I said. "Not really. I mean, I was, but not anymore."

Then Alison started talking to Jeanne, and Mrs. Stricker told us to move toward the exit, and the whole thing just kind of went *pffffft*.

Oh well. Better luck next tragedy.

STOP AND GO

We got to have lunch outside again that day. This time it was on the South Bank, which is basically a giant, long park along the Thames River.

There was a ton of cool stuff to see, like a graffitied-up skateboard park, people painting by the river, and some people who *were* art, like human statues who only moved if you put money in their box.

There were musicians, too—all kinds of people making money and making art at the same time. Ms. Donatello said they were called buskers. It was super-cool.

Inspiring, even. That's what my mom would say.

So I decided to put the whole Jeanne tragedy in the backseat and keep moving forward. When we started eating lunch, Jeanne sat next to me.

"What next?" she asked.

"Actually, I have an idea I want to try, and this would be a great spot for it," I said.

"Come on, Jeanne," Jared said. "Let's go buy a T-shirt or something."

"No, I want to do this with Rafe," she said.

Jared looked at her, and then evil-eyed me some more. Then he put on that fake smile of his.

"Yeah, okay," he said. "What are we doing?"

I wanted to tell Jared to jump in the Thames and wait for further instructions, but that wasn't going to happen. Besides, I needed at least a couple of people for this.

"Why don't you guys stand over there?" I said as we put down our food.

I got them lined up with the river in the background. Then I took out my phone.

"Now stand really still, but like you're running," I said.

My idea was this thing called stop motion. The way you do it is, you turn on the camera and record for maybe half a second. Then you pause it, and the people move, but just a little bit.

Then you unpause, and record for half a second, and repause. Then they move again.

Over and over and over.

It's like making a human cartoon, and it looks really cool if you do it right.

And here's another thing. You know what happens when super-popular people start doing whatever you're doing? Other people get interested.

In fact, we'd barely even started before Sabra and Katrina came over.

"What are you guys doing?" Katrina said.

"Making a video," Jeanne said.

"Ooh, fun! Can we be in it?" Sabra asked, even though if *I'd* asked her to do it, she probably would have laughed my face off.

"Sure," Jeanne said. "Where do you want them, Rafe?"

"Katrina, go stand right there," I said. "Sabra, stand next to her. Jared and Jeanne, stay right where you are, and look surprised."

Half a second later, it was like Katrina and Sabra had just popped up into the scene from out of nowhere. And we kept going from there.

Pretty soon, almost everyone in the class was getting into it. Including Jared. I kept popping people in and out, making it up as I went along—and making something pretty cool, if I do say so myself. Even the other tourists were stopping and watching, like we were part of that whole London art scene.

Which I guess we kind of were.

WE
WE LONDON

CHAPTER 35

EYE SPY

When we got in line for the London Eye, I was excited…and nervous.

And excited.

But mostly nervous.

The London Eye was like an enormous Ferris wheel, but instead of benches it had big see-through pod-things. I didn't know if getting way up there in those glass pods was going to be like standing inside a tall building, which I could deal with. Or maybe it was going to be more like hanging off the edge of a cliff, which I definitely couldn't.

If you read my story about last summer in the Rockies, then you already know that the whole edge-of-a-cliff thing makes me get dizzy and sweaty and panicky and at least a little bit throw-uppy. It's not pretty.

But, on the other hand, I knew I could get some amazing shots of London from up there. I didn't want to miss out. And I definitely didn't want to look like Rafe Khatchadorian: International Chicken in front of the whole class.

Besides, this was nothing compared to the Rocky Mountains. Right?

So I decided to go for it.

Those pods were big enough for twenty-five people, and we were split into two groups. Jeanne and Jared went one way. I went the other. Jared seemed like he'd had enough of *The Rafe & Jeanne Show* for one day, and I didn't want to push my luck with him. I just wanted to focus on getting some great video.

"Welcome to the London Eye," a recording said. "Please step all the way in and mind the closing doors."

Okay, I thought, breathing in slowly. *Here goes nothing*.

And speaking of nothing, that's what I got when I pulled out my phone. All that stop-motion stuff we'd been doing had run the battery down to zilch.

I turned around fast, but the doors had already closed. Now I was headed up, up, up, and around with a dead camera in my hand, and there wasn't anything I could do about it.

Or…was there?

I worked fast. I dug into my backpack and pulled out the assignment sheet. Then I checked to see who was supposed to take pictures of this thing. Of course, with the classic Khatchadorian luck, it was *him.*

"Hey, Miller?" I said. "Can I use your camera?"

"Yeah, right," Miller said. "Like I'm going to trust you with a brand-new MyPhone 10 Deluxe."

"Please?" I said. "I'll do your photography assignment."

That actually got him interested. He thought about it for a second, then pulled out his phone and punched in the passcode.

"Just remember," he said, "you break it—"

"I know, I know—I bought it," I said.

"Yeah," he said. "But I break *you, too.*"

"Fair enough," I said.

Then I went to the middle of the pod, sat down on the bench, and tried to get used to the idea that this thing was only going higher before it got any lower.

I took another deep breath. *No problem,* I thought. *I can do this.*

And even if I couldn't, it wasn't like I had much choice now. I was in it.

It took me a while, but I figured out that if I kept breathing and didn't look straight down over the edge, it wasn't *quite* as bad as it could have been.

Also, that whole huge view of the city (which was AWESOME, by the way) looked way smaller on the phone's screen. So I stayed laser-focused on that. Everything was just a little better-looking through the camera. And then, just when it seemed like we were getting to the tippy-top of the world and I was sort of, almost getting comfortable—*PING!* Miller's phone went off.

I looked over at him, but he was too busy checking the view to notice. Then I looked down and saw there was a text notification on his screen. The text was from "Mom," but all I could see were the first few words.

If I wanted to know any more, I had to tap on the message. Which was a very tempting thought.

It was also a terrible idea. And the reason I know is because I thought, *This is a terrible idea*—right before I did it anyway.

Maybe it was the altitude. Maybe my curiosity got the best of me. Maybe I'm just an idiot.

Who knows? But I'll tell you this much. I sure wasn't expecting what I found out next.

Dryden—I just got word from Xavier Academy. You will start there on the first of the month!

Isn't that wonderful? ☺

Believe me, Chunkins, you are going to love living in Phoenix.

Promise!!

Love, Mom

It was like every molecule in my brain fired at once.

HO.

LY.

SMOKES!

Miller was *MOVING?* To *Phoenix??*

Not to mention...*Chunkins???* And I thought Dryden was bad, but...wow.

This was why Miller had been crying on the first night, wasn't it? Because he was moving—far, far away.

But not yet. Because when I looked up, Miller was coming right at me.

"Are you using that camera or not?" he asked.

"YES!" I said, kind of weirdly loud. Then I walked over to the pod wall and started filming again before I had to look him in the eye even one more second.

After that, my hands kind of took over for me. They went back to making the video on their own, while my brain flipped, and flopped, and twisted around just trying to have all the thoughts it was having. Because—

This. Changed. Everything.

POP ~~QUIZ~~ MEETING

Once I came back down to earth (in more ways than one), I figured my best option with Miller was to keep doing nothing. I mean, this was huger than huge, for sure. But I wasn't going to tell "Dryden" that I'd just read his text any more than I was going to tell him that I heard all that crying on the first night. Things between me and Miller had gotten all the way up to not-completely-horrible by now. I wanted it to keep going that way if I could.

Besides, as soon as we pulled up to the hotel that night, Mrs. Stricker dropped another whole pile of *uh-oh* in my lap.

"Report Committee, we will have a short status meeting in the Learning Center before curfew," she said.

"Does that mean *now?*" I asked.

"Yes, now," Stricker said.

I looked right over at Jeanne. This was like a pop quiz. I hadn't had any chance to figure out what we were doing next, or what the new assignments were, or any of the stuff Mrs. Stricker *thought* I knew how to do.

I guess I could have tried to wing it, but...who am I kidding? There was NO WAY I could wing something like that.

"What do I say?" I asked Jeanne while we were walking through the lobby.

"Just..." She was thinking fast, I could tell. "Just say that everyone is going to switch jobs tomorrow. The writers will do photography and the photographers will do the writing."

"That's good," I said. It was something I could actually remember.

"Oh, and if Mrs. Stricker asks, we hit three of our topics today," Jeanne said. "Isaiah got a bunch of stuff from Sabra and Kadir on the Saatchi, and I asked Mackenzie to focus on the history of the Old Globe—"

"Whoa-whoa-whoa!" I said. "Too much information!"

"Well, she's going to want to know," Jeanne said. "And it's supposed to come from you."

"I know, I know," I said, frantically trying to keep everything Jeanne said from leaking out of my brain.

We were heading up the hall now, away from the front desk and right toward the Learning Center.

"I've got it!" Jeanne said. "Keep your phone where you can see it. I'll text you the rest."

"But my phone's dead!" I said. "I have to charge it first."

"There's no time for that!" she said.

It was like a countdown to disaster, and *I* was the bomb that was going to go off in about twelve and a half seconds.

"Unless—," Jeanne said.

"Unless what?" I said.

"Let's go, you two!" Mrs. Stricker said. She was standing in the Learning Center door, looking like she couldn't wait to get upstairs, order room service, and watch some TV. Or whatever it is she does for fun.

"Here! Take this," Jeanne said. She shoved her phone into my hand. "Open the text window and turn it on mute."

"But...," I said.

"Just do it!" Jeanne said.

So I did. There wasn't much choice, anyway. We were already walking into the room and that meeting was about to start in five...four...three... two...

COVERT OPERATIONS

"Ms. Donatello, may I use your laptop to take notes?" Jeanne asked, once we were all sitting at the big table in the Learning Center.

"Of course," Ms. Donatello said, and slid it over to her.

"Okay, everyone, it's been a long day. Let's make this quick," Mrs. Stricker said.

I still didn't know where this was headed. Everyone else was getting their notebooks out, but Jeanne was already tapping away on Ms. D's laptop.

And then a text popped up on her phone.

ARE YOU GETTING THIS?
SCRATCH YOUR HEAD FOR YES.

I scratched my head and kind of glanced over at Jeanne. She just kept typing away, like she didn't even know I was there.

"All right, Rafe," Mrs. Stricker said. "What's our plan for tomorrow?"

At least I was ready for that one.

"I think we should switch what we did today," I said. "Everyone who did written modules can take pictures tomorrow, and everyone who took pictures can do the write-ups."

"That's a very elegant plan," Ms. Donatello said. "I'm impressed, Rafe."

"Thanks," I said. It made me feel good but also guilty, since Jeanne deserved the credit.

Meanwhile, I was hoping like crazy that would be it, because I was already out of stuff to say. But Mrs. Stricker kept going.

"Now remember, you'll continue posting individual updates to the school website," she said. "But we need to make sure all topic areas are covered in the Living-Learning entry we submit at the end of the week. How is that coming along, Rafe?"

"Well," I said, "let me just, uh…check my notes."

I flipped through a few pages in my notebook and pretended to read them, while Jeanne kept tapping away, eventually stammering, “Uh…hang on two or ten seconds…” And then—

WE HAVE A GOOD START ON HISTORY, ART, AND CURRENT EVENTS

Phew!

“We have a good start on history, art, and current events,” I said.

POLITICS AND SCIENCE WILL GET CAUGHT UP TOMORROW

“Politics and science will get caught up tomorrow,” I said.

AND BY THE END OF THE WEEK WE SHOULD BE FUNNY CORNERED

“And by the end of the week we should be funny cornered,” I said.

"Excuse me?" Mrs. Stricker said, and everyone looked up.

FULLY COVERED!!! (SORRY!)

"Fully covered!" I said. "I mean…fully covered!" Stupid autocorrect! I don't know if Jeanne was sweating like me, but I felt like I was drowning.

Mrs. Stricker just stared back at me. It was like she could *smell* something was wrong, but she couldn't tell what it was. (And believe me, she can smell trouble.) Everything else stopped—including my heart, I think.

Then she finally stood up.

"You all have one hour before curfew. Please have your latest materials loaded onto the HVMS site by then. I'll be checking your progress from my room," she said, and flipped her laptop closed on her way out the door.

When I looked over at Jeanne, she didn't look sweaty at all. In fact, I think she was ready for Round Two.

Not me. I felt like I'd just starred in all the *Mission: Impossible* movies at the same time. And the only reason I'd made it out alive was thanks to Special Agent Galletta.

Also known as Jeanne.

Which, if you ask me, must be short for *genius.*

CRAZY DANGEROUS

By the time I got up to the room that night, I was *beat*. I felt like a wrung-out washrag after a double shift at the 24-hour car wash. All I wanted to do was crawl into a nice comfortable bed and go to sleep for eight or twenty hours.

Of course, I also wanted a lifetime supply of pepperoni pizza, world peace, and Bill Gates's ATM card, but I wasn't getting any of those, either.

When I walked in, Miller flicked his light off right away, even though he wasn't going to sleep. He was still watching TV on top of the covers.

"What's up?" I said.

"Nnrh," he said, which I think meant "Nothing."

"You want some Cadbury?" I asked him, and held up a candy bar I bought in the lobby.

"Nah," he said.

And that's when I knew he was feeling worse than ever. Miller likes food more than I do.

I figured he must be pretty depressed about moving to Phoenix, but I couldn't tell *him* that.

"Hey, Miller?" I said. "You, uh...you don't seem so good."

This time, he didn't say anything. He just kept watching TV, even though it was only a commercial for something called potted meat (whatever that is).

"Miller?" I said again.

"I don't want to talk about it," he said.

"Talk about *what?*" I said. "What's going on?"

I could tell things had changed between us, because I was saying stuff that would have put me in the obituaries back home. And Miller didn't even *pretend* like he cared.

So I kept going.

"You just seem like you wish you'd never come to London," I said.

"Good call, Sherlock," he said, and turned up the TV.

"Okay, whatever," I said. "I'll see you in the morning."

And I was halfway to my bedroom-in-the-bathroom when I got another idea. A big one. Kind of crazy, too. Like, almost Leo-the-Silent crazy. But I figured it was time to try something new.

So I stopped and turned around. I walked over to the dresser, where Miller kept his never-ending pile of junk food. And then I started putting some chips and cans of soda into my backpack.

It felt like I was taking my life into my own hands, because I kind of was. But it snapped Miller out of whatever had him lying there like a zombie. As soon as he saw me going for his food, he launched off that bed like an enemy missile.

"What do you think you're doing?" he snarled. "Are you crazy?"

"Yeah," I said, looking him right in the eye while I dropped another bag of Walkers crisps in there. "A little, anyway."

I'm pretty sure he pulled back his fist to send me through the wall, but I had my eyes locked on his. This was a do-or-die moment—probably with extra emphasis on the *die*.

"Come on," I said, trying to sound at least a little like I wasn't shaking in my socks. "Let's hit the roof again. And this time, we're bringing some supplies."

CHAPTER 39

OPERATION: BABY STEPS

Believe it or not, it worked. I think Miller liked that first mission up to the roof a lot. In fact, that's what I was counting on.

So as soon as curfew kicked in and Security Guy was out of the way, we went for it. In fact, it wasn't nearly as hard the second time around. We got up to that roof faster than you can say "stealth mode." There wasn't even any tape on our doors—maybe our group had worked up some sort of trust with Security Guy already. Either that or he was just plain lazy.

This time, we pulled one of those restaurant tables and a couple of folding chairs to the middle of the roof. Then we sat back and relaxed with a table full of Miller's junk food. He even let me eat a little of it. Which was, frankly, amazing.

And then came Part Two of my plan. If it had a name, I'd call it Operation: Baby Steps.

"Hey, Miller, I didn't mean to be nosy before," I said.

Miller finished chugging a can of orange soda and popped a Coke.

"Whatever," he said.

"You just don't seem like you're having any fun," I said. "None of my friends are here, either. I get it."

"No, actually, you don't," Miller said. He seemed like he was heading down into the dumps again, so I didn't say anything. I just drank my warm Coke and watched the city lights.

Then after a long time, Miller spoke up again.

"It's my little sister," he said.

I didn't know what he meant, but it felt like something had just changed. Maybe something big. It reminded me of when you see those giant icebergs breaking off from themselves—kind of surprising and scary at the same time.

"What about her?" I said.

"She has to go to this clinic in Phoenix," he said.

"For what?" I asked him.

Then he named something I'd never heard of. It sounded to me like the biggest word Miller had ever used.

"Does that mean she's sick?" I asked. Miller just shrugged, but I think that meant yes.

It made me want to tell him about Leo, and how I had a sick brother, once. But then I stopped and thought about it for a second. Seeing as how Leo died, maybe that wasn't such a good thing to talk about after all. Even if it did happen a long time ago.

"I bet she'll be okay," I said instead. "That clinic must be really good or your parents wouldn't take her all the way down there."

"Yeah," Miller said.

To tell you the truth, I still wasn't sorry Miller was moving to Phoenix. But I was definitely less glad about it than before.

He didn't say anything else, and I was pretty sure the conversation was over. But I wasn't done yet. I still had my backpack with me, and I pulled out the assignment sheet for the next day. Then I took out my pencil and erased Miller's name.

"What are you doing?" he said.

"I'm taking you off the assignment sheet for tomorrow," I said. "I mean, you probably don't care or anything, but it sounds like you could use a day off from that stuff."

All I heard then was Miller swallowing hard in the dark. Which made me feel 100 percent weird—for both our sakes. Or maybe he just had an extra-big chip in his mouth, I don't know.

"Hey, Rafe?" he said.

"Yeah?" I said.

"Thanks," he said. "I owe you one."

"Don't worry about it," I told him.

And I even meant it. I was supposed to be doing nice things for people. Be friendly, right? Even to Dryden Miller.

Especially to Miller, now.

DAY FOUR IN LONDON

Hey there, all you readers, and viewers, and listeners, and fans! Welcome to Day Four in London.

Are you READY???? I hope so, because it's time to play everyone's favorite game...

HERE'S HOW IT'S PLAYED.

1. Leave the hotel first thing after breakfast.
2. Walk right past the place where the bus usually parks. You won't be needing it.
3. On today's agenda, we have the National Portrait Gallery, Changing of the Guard at Buckingham Palace, Hyde Park, the Houses of Parliament, and everything in between. **Total miles: too many to count!**
4. Anyone who makes it to the end of the day alive... **WINS!**
5. **Bonus points** if you finish without blisters, limping, falling behind, or complaining.
6. **Helpful Hint:** Nobody earns bonus points.
7. Comfortable shoes required.
8. Oxygen not included.
9. **READY? Set! WALK!!!**

HYDE PARK PLACE
PARK STREET
THE LONG WATER
W. CARRIAGE DRIVE
THE SERPENTINE
Hyde Park

COVENT GARDEN
National Portrait GALLERY
STRAND
THAMES
PALL MALL
BIG BEN
BUCKINGHAM PALACE
THE MALL
ST. JAMES PARK
10 DOWNING STREET
BIRDCAGE WALK
HOUSES OF Parliament
VICTORIA ST.

TROUBLE ON THE TUBE

By the time we left the National Portrait Gallery, everyone was pretty much walked out. I'd gotten some great video and some not-so-great video.

I'd also spent nearly the rest of my money on presents for Mom, Grandma, and even Georgia. Plus the biggest Cadbury bar you've ever seen (for me).

But the best part was still coming. Our last stop of the afternoon was going to be Madame Fifi's House of Wax. And to make it even better, we got to ride there on the subway and take a bus back to the hotel afterward. I'm pretty sure if we had to walk anymore, everyone would have been going home on crutches.

I've lived in a city before, but I've never ridden on a subway. In London, it's called the Tube, which is a cool name, if you ask me. It's like a whole huge underground maze that goes everywhere.

When we got on the train, I didn't fight anyone for a seat. I was still trying to do nice things and be friendly, so I held on to a pole instead, and tried not to stand on my blisters.

Then, when we were almost to Madame Fifi's, Jared came over to where I was standing. I didn't know what he wanted, but I had a hunch it wasn't about starring in my next movie.

"What's up, Rafe?" he said, flashing that weird smile.

"Nothing," I said, because he wasn't really asking.

"You and Jeanne have been getting a lot of stuff done for that report," he said, "haven't you?"

"Yeah," I said. "It's been pretty great."

"Pretty great?" he said. "She's not your girlfriend. You know that, right?"

That wasn't a real question, either, but I knew where he was going.

"Don't worry, Jared," I told him. "It's not like—"

“Oh, I’m not worried,” he said. “I’m just saying, you got the help you needed. Now maybe you could stop crushing on *my* girlfriend and leave her alone. Cool?”

Jeanne was way across the subway car, but I could see her looking at us with this question on her face, like—*What are they up to?*

Jared just smiled and waved at her. That smile of his was getting creepier by the second.

And I didn't even answer him this time. We were pulling into our stop at Waterloo Station. Plus, it was starting to hit my brain what was really going on with all the fake smiles and questions. Or at least, what *might* have been going on.

FACT: Jared was taller than me, better-looking than me, and pretty much better at everything than I was.

FACT: He didn't have any reason to be jealous of me, but he sure was acting that way.

THEORY: Jared actually WAS jealous.

CONCLUSION: The world had gone completely insane.

WELCOME TO MADAME FIFI'S HOUSE OF WAX

I'd already seen a brochure for Madame Fifi's back at the hotel. Not only did the main exhibit of wax figures sound pretty cool—Barack Obama! Darth Vader! Beyoncé!—but I was even more excited about the basement.

Because that's where they had Madame Fifi's Temple of Terrors, and all the gory stuff. In other words, all the good stuff. Where else were you going to see beheadings, guys on spikes, people on the rack, *and* a fully stocked gift shop? It was going to be like walking into a living horror movie with overpriced knickknacks at the end!

Which meant that this video was practically going to make itself.

Our tour guide this time was a lady called Ms. Evelyn. Except she said it like "Eve-Lynn." She also wore this long dress and a turban on her head, like some kind of really old movie star who over… pronounced…every…word…she…ever…said.

"Welcome…welcome…welcome," she told us (which took about an hour to say), and I knew right then I was going to have to be patient.

Ms. Evelyn started off by taking us around the ground-floor exhibit. Besides all the movie and sports people, there were a bunch of wax dummies of people from history. And of course, she told us all about them, too.

I got some good video, though. We saw everyone from Prince the musician to the Prince of Wales, and Elton John to Genghis Khan. (Hey, I'm a poet!) Jeanne kept giving me looks when Mrs. Stricker wasn't watching, so I'd know which parts made sense to focus on.

And Jared kept giving me looks, too, when Jeanne wasn't watching. I tried to ignore him, and I made sure to keep my distance from him *and* Jeanne.

The whole time, Ms. Evelyn was gliding around and talking (and talking and talking), while the rest of us were getting as impatient as little kids on Christmas Eve. Either she didn't know that everyone was goofing off behind her back during the tour, or she didn't care.

Or maybe she had it all figured out. Maybe she knew all that grinning and goofing off was going to stop the very minute we headed down to the basement.

If that's what she thought, she was exactly right.

When we finally got to the main entrance for the Temple of Terrors, Ms. Evelyn stopped cold. Like a dead body.

Then she looked at all of us, one by one, and her eyes got really big and spooky.

"I hope you have...*prepared* yourselves," she said.

"Yes!" everyone basically yelled at the same time in anticipation. My voice didn't even crack, which was like a little present, from me to me. (Thanks, voice!)

"Very well, then," she said, and opened this big door to show us some winding stairs, down into the dark.

But before she could lead us down them, she stopped and turned around again.

"There's nobody in the group with a...weak heart?" she asked.

"No!" almost everyone said.

"All right, then," Ms. Evelyn said. "But please... don't say I didn't *warn* you."

She was totally putting on a show, if you ask me. And yeah, it was totally working, because I was a little bit nervous by then. Maybe more than a little bit.

I think everyone else was, too, because the whole group got pretty quiet and tense after that.

When I looked over at Miller, he seemed like he didn't want to be there. But that could have meant anything.

"Scared?" I asked him.

"Shut up," he said.

Yeah, we were *totally* like best buds now.

So I pointed my phone camera straight ahead and kept on going. You know those movie scenes where it's like the camera *is* someone? All you can see is what that character sees, and maybe you just hear them breathing?

That's what I was going for. It was like letting whoever watched the video go on the tour with us. And see whatever we were going to see.

So come on. Step right this way...if you dare.

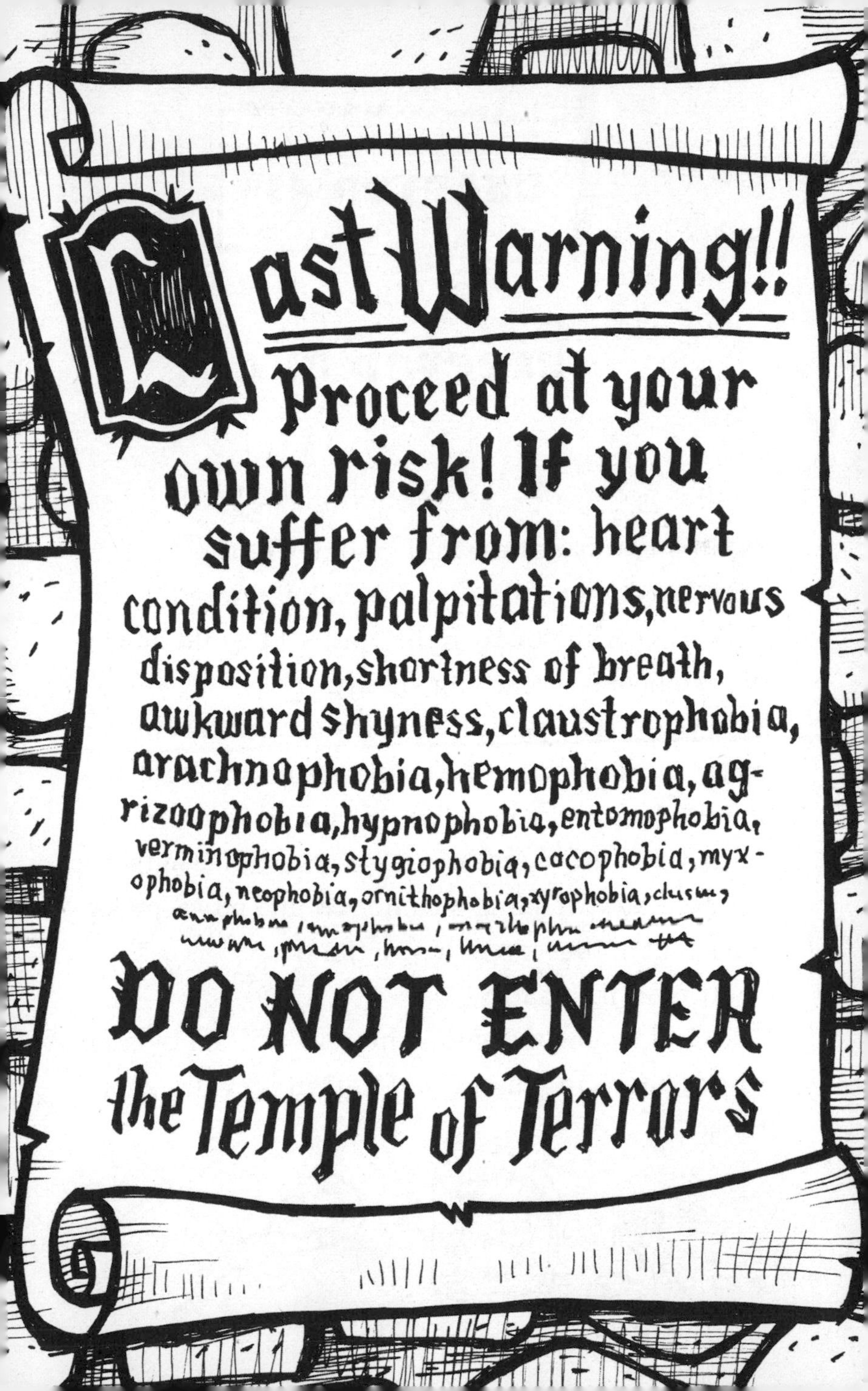
Last Warning!!
Proceed at your own risk! If you suffer from: heart condition, palpitations, nervous disposition, shortness of breath, awkward shyness, claustrophobia, arachnophobia, hemophobia, agrizoophobia, hypnophobia, entomophobia, verminophobia, stygiophobia, cacophobia, myxophobia, neophobia, ornithophobia, xyrophobia,
DO NOT ENTER
the Temple of Terrors

CHAPTER 43

CREEPED OUT

It was way darker and smokier in the basement. All I could see ahead was this flickering, dim yellow light, and all I could hear was someone screaming shrilly.

I was *like 87 percent* sure it was just fake torches, a dry-ice machine, and a sound recording. But you know when you're in bed at night and you're *about 87 percent* sure there isn't a crazed maniac outside your window wielding a chainsaw and a face mask made out of the skin of his victims?

It was like that.

"Cool," someone said, when we walked by a long row of heads in glass jars. I definitely got a shot of those.

The farther in we went, the more crowded it got. There were fake people getting executed and fake people who had already died. Also, executioners, famous murderers, and a bunch of other people you'd never want to meet.

I think the creepiest part was the way all of it *wasn't* just from a movie. This was stuff that had really happened, in real life. And some of those wax dummies had eyes that followed you wherever you went.

Like Vlad the Impaler, whose name kind of speaks for itself.

And Jack the Ripper, who terrorized London in Victorian times and thankfully wasn't around to murder us all now.

And Madame Elizabeth Bathory. Guess what she liked to take a bath in? (Hint: It's not hot, perfumed water and frothy bubbles. More Obvious Hint: It was BLOOD!) I got a great shot of that display, too, right down to the slightly pink towels.

"That...is...*awesome!*" Jeanne said, looking over my shoulder. But she was also whisper-imitating Ms. Evelyn.

"I...love...*corpses!*" I whispered back, and we

both cracked up. We'd have to cut that part out of the video, but oh well.

"Do you think we're getting everything we need?" Jeanne asked.

"I think so," I said. "But I'm down to fumes on my phone battery."

"Here. Use mine again," she said.

"Uhh, I don't know," I said.

"Why not?" Jeanne said, and gave me her phone to take. I didn't know how to say no, so I took it—

Right before I turned around and saw the scariest dummy of them all.

Maybe it was the fake torchlight, but I swear, Jared looked just like one of those wax killers. (And I don't mean the waxy part.)

"Hey, Jeanne," he said, even though he was looking at me. "Come over here. There's something I want to show you."

"Okay," she said. "See you later, Rafe?"

"Sure," I said. But I heard a little bit of what they said before they walked away.

"Why does he need your phone?" Jared asked her.

"Because his battery ran out," Jeanne said.

"Yeah, right," Jared said.

"What's that supposed to mean?" Jeanne asked.

I didn't hear any more after that. So I just went back to focusing on the dead people, killers, and creeps down there in the basement.

Besides Jared, I mean.

AND THEN...

By the end of the tour, I think everyone was kind of worn out from being so scared. I got a bunch of great stuff, though. Right up until Jeanne's phone died, too, and I gave it back to her.

"Thank you, thank you, this is our last tour of the day," Ms. Evelyn said. I noticed she was talking a lot faster, too. "If you wouldn't mind proceeding to the exit, thank you, thank you..."

"Excuse me, ma'am," I asked her, "is there a bathroom I can use?"

"Loos are back downstairs on the left, love," she said. "Just past the main torture chamber."

There was a bus outside to pick us up, and everyone was still filing out that way, so I ran down real quick, back into the dark. I tried to shake off that feeling like someone was watching me, but it wasn't so easy. Not with all those glass eyes everywhere.

I hustled past one door marked WITCHES and opened the next one, marked WARLOCKS. It was a relief to just get in there and turn on a real light.

But then, I was halfway unzipped, and I heard this loud *click* behind me. Then a *thud* and a shuffling sound from outside the bathroom door.

"What was that?" I said, even though I was alone. Unless you count Leo the Silent, which I was starting to do, pretty quick.

I still had to go to the bathroom, but I went back over and tried to open the door.

Tried. Did you catch that? It's important.

Someone—or some ghost of some crazed psycho killer from hundreds of years ago—had just locked me in the loo.

I was trapped.

Right by the torture chambers where dozens of creepy wax killers and corpses were posed.

Yes. For real.

Gulp!

HELLLLLLLP!!!!!

Oh man.

Oh man.

Ohhhhhh man.

Okay, you might think this is the craziest part of all, but before I did anything else, I did what I'd come down there to do. The only other option was wetting my pants. Can you imagine if I showed up on that bus with a dark stain where my zipper was?

Nope. No way, I thought. *Let the ghost of Vlad the Impaler take me instead.*

So I did my business as fast as humanly possible and then went back to pounding on the bathroom door.

Oh man.

Oh man.

Ohhhhhh man.

"Leo, what do I do?" I said. I was seriously panicking now. I've already told you about my "active" imagination, right? That's a good thing, most of the time. But it can also work against you.

For a second, I thought about calling someone. But then I remembered I couldn't.

"Grandma Dotty has *got* to get a new phone," Leo said. "That thing must be six years old."

"*That's* what you're thinking about?" I said. "We need to find a way out of here."

"I'm just saying, with a dead phone—"

"DON'T SAY *DEAD!*" I said.

I'm not sure how long it went on. A lifetime? Two minutes? Somewhere in between?

But then something rattled on the other side of the door, and I jumped back. When it started to open, I might have even screamed, too. Was I about to be saved, or meet my gut-ripping fate?

And yeah, maybe I was being a little dramatic. But try getting locked in a Temple of Terrors bathroom sometime and see what kinds of tricks your mind plays on *you*.

Even when I saw the security guard standing there, I wasn't completely done feeling freaked out.

"What in the world?" the guard said. He was holding a chair in one hand and the doorknob with the other. "Looks like you got pranked, young man. And not a very funny prank at that."

"Is my bus still here?" I yelled.

"Sorry, don't know," he said. "I'm just here to close up for the night."

"What?" I said. "What time is it?"

He looked at his watch. "Ten to five," he said.

I'd only been in there a couple of minutes. That was great news—but I didn't have any time to lose.

"Thanksforlettingmeout!" I said, and took off running up the stairs.

The lobby was empty when I got there, and the lights were off. There was no sign of Ms. Evelyn or anyone, but maybe they were all waiting for me outside. I pushed through the front door, ran out onto the sidewalk, and—

No bus. No Mrs. Stricker. No nothing.

Just me.

Lost in London.

CHAPTER 46

(NOT) HERE!

O*kay,* I thought. *Don't panic.*

Really. Don't panic, I thought.

It didn't work. I was totally panicking.

The door to Madame Fifi's had just locked behind me, and no one answered when I pounded on it. I was standing there by myself, *somewhere* in the middle of London.

Did I have any money in my pockets? No, I did not.

Did I have a working phone? No, I did not.

Did I know where the hotel was? No, I did not.

And even though none of this was my fault, something told me Mrs. Stricker wasn't going to care about that. In fact, she told me so, right after the whole crown jewels disaster.

"Don't worry," Leo told me. "We've got this."

"What do I do?" I said.

"Back to the riverbank?" he suggested. I'd just spotted a sign for South Bank, and that was as good as anything. At least it was somewhere I'd been before.

So I followed the signs—real ones this time.

The more I walked, the more I figured out the whole story. First of all, *someone* had locked me in that bathroom. And you could bet that someone's name started with an *M* or a *J*.

For *Miller*. Or *Jared*.

And either way, that was only half the story. I was pretty sure the second half went something like this:

Then Mrs. Stricker put a check by my name, the bus took off, and nobody even noticed I was missing.

The only thing was, it didn't add up when I thought about it. I mean, I knew Jared pretty much hated me. But I thought Miller and I were actually doing okay. He even said he owed me one.

Whatever. I couldn't worry about all that right now, I had to focus.

Survival mode: ON.

The only option was to figure out a way back, hopefully faster than the bus. Then I could hang around outside the hotel and wait for them to show up. Yeah, that was it—I'd stay out of sight, like maybe behind a big plant, and when everyone started filing off the bus, I'd just fall into line—

Oh wait. That's another movie. Never mind.

What I needed was a ride. A city bus would be cheap, if I knew which one to take. Which I didn't.

But a taxi could get me there. The question was, how much would that cost? Because I had exactly zero pounds and zero change in my pocket.

So then, how quick could I get the cash? And could I really earn it in the way I was starting to think just might work?

"Sure you can," Leo said.

Maybe, I thought.

But there was only one way to find out.

When I got to the river, there were tons of people around. No ghosts, or flesh-eaters, or wax murderers—just regular tourists, buskers, that kind of thing. Perfect.

I found an empty spot where I could sit on a bench. Then I opened my backpack and pulled out my sketch pad and pen.

I took a deep breath. This was something I could do, but I was still kind of scared to try it.

"Just go for it," Leo said. "This is awesome."

"Easy for you to say," I told him. "I'm the one who's going to spend the rest of his life in middle school."

"Not helping," Leo said. "You can do this, Khatchadorian. NOW!"

So I drew a picture of the first person I could think of. Jeanne Galletta. She was fresh in my memory, anyway, and it was better than advertising with a picture of Vlad the Impaler.

When it was done, I wrote PORTRAITS, THREE POUNDS at the top of the page.

Was that the right price? I had no idea. Would it be enough to get me a taxi back to the hotel? Hopefully.

So as the next wave of tourists walked by, I took another deep breath and held up my drawing.

Then I called out, nice and clear, "Would anyone like their portrait drawn?"

I was officially open for business.

DRAWING ON MY EXPERIENCE

Here's the amazing thing. It actually worked. Not right away, but after asking about twenty people if they wanted a drawing of themselves, someone said yes.

And then someone else after that. So even though I was still nervous about Mrs. Stricker, I also started getting into it. I'm not saying they were going to hang my stuff in the National Portrait Gallery, but it *was* the first time I got paid for my artwork.

Once I'd done a couple of drawings for three pounds, I told the next lady it was five pounds, and she didn't even blink. She asked if I could draw her and her daughter next to Big Ben, and I said no sweat. She even paid me double, since there were two of them—ten pounds!

"Here you go," she said, handing me the money. "My daughter says you're very dreamy, with that sketch pad and those lovely eyes of yours."

"Mum!" the girl said. She seemed like she was just as embarrassed as I was. Except, I think it was *bad* embarrassed for her, and a tiny bit good embarrassed for me, if you know what I mean.

Either way, I just turned red and started packing up my stuff. It was time to go.

I didn't know it yet, but all this was the easy part. Next, I had to find a cab, figure out how to make it stop for me, hope the driver knew where the hotel was, pray that I had enough money to get there…

And *then* deal with the hard part.

Also known as Principal Ida P. Stricker.

CHAPTER 48

HOTEL, SWEET HOTEL

By the time my cab pulled up in front of the hotel (fourteen pounds and thirty-five pence—I told the driver to keep the change), I was feeling kind of numb. Especially my feet—I think I walked about eighteen miles that day.

Also, I didn't really know what to expect next.

The lobby was practically full when I walked inside. I saw a couple of policemen and a bunch of people from the hotel. Mrs. Stricker was talking on the phone, and Ms. Donatello was the first one to see me.

"There he is!" she said.

It was like I'd just turned into some kind of human magnet, because everyone came at me at once.

Okay, maybe there weren't any cameras or reporters, but it sure felt that way, with all the questions.

"Are you okay, son?"

"What happened?"

"How did you get back?"

"WHERE...WERE...YOU?!"

That last one was Mrs. Stricker, in case you couldn't guess. She was at the head of the pack, and that's when I knew it was all over for me. I was about to get the biggest F of my life.

But then, just as fast, I thought of something else. And I realized maybe it didn't have to go that way.

So I answered the questions with a question.

"What happened?" I said, trying my best to look scared, which wasn't that hard after everything that happened.

"That's what I'm asking *you!*" Mrs. Stricker said.

"Well..." I looked around at everyone looking back at me. And I took my time. "One minute I was in the bathroom," I said, "and the next, everyone was just gone. You left me behind!"

I wasn't going to say anything about Miller or Jared. The whole idea right now was to simplify this, not make it more complicated.

"But you answered at roll call!" Mrs. Stricker said. "It's right here!" She even held up her list so I could see where my name was checked off.

"Except, he couldn't have," Ms. Donatello said loudly. "Because he wasn't on the bus."

And everyone went from looking at me…back to Mrs. Stricker.

"But...but…well…," Mrs. Stricker said. "Rafe, I am…so…sss..."

Now she looked like she was going to throw up.

"I am so…sor…ry," she said. "You must have… been very brave."

I took a big breath and let it out. I was relieved, but not in the way they thought.

"I'm just really glad to be back safe," I said, and looked at the ground. "I was pretty scared when I realized I was all alone in this big city."

What can I say? I was totally milking it. I know that doesn't make me a better person, but I didn't feel too guilty about it, either. You know what they say about desperate times calling for desperate measures, right?

And besides, Mrs. Stricker really did leave me behind. And it really wasn't my fault. That's just the truth.

So I'm sticking to it.

A NIGHT (NOT) ON THE TOWN

I got in trouble with Mrs. Stricker anyway. Even if she didn't put it that way.

Once everything had settled down, she came over to talk to me again. And it started out with, "I think it would be best for you if..."

Okay, time out! When an adult says that, there's maybe a fifty-fifty chance it's *actually* going to be something that's best for you. We all know that, right? Half the time, it's all about what they want.

Which I guess is why I got left back that night. So while everyone else went to see a musical at the National Theatre, I ate dinner with Mr. Chin at the hotel so I could "get some rest."

Basically, that's what you call an in-hotel suspension.

On the downside, I was missing everything that night, and it was all Miller's fault. Or Jared's. I also had to listen to Andrea Chin's dad talk *all* about his job running a human resources department at a law firm.

But on the upside? Well, I guess I got that rest I was supposed to have.

MY MIND, OFFICIALLY BLOWN

Everyone got back later than curfew. I was already in my room, watching people play darts on TV, when Miller came in. He actually looked kind of pumped.

"Man, everyone was talking about you," he said.

"Yeah," I said, "I'll bet."

I didn't want to pick a fight, but I was pretty ticked off. I mean, if Miller was actually the one who locked me in the bathroom, that really stank.

But it didn't take long for me to find out otherwise.

"Jeanne made Jared tell Mrs. Stricker about what he did to you," Miller said.

"She did?"

"Yeah. So you're off the hook."

"I am?" I said.

"Yeah," Miller said, looking at me like—*duh*. "I mean, it was a pretty good stunt, if you ask me. But it's not like they were just going to let that one slide."

"Wow," I said. I guess that meant Jared was the one in trouble now. And I never even had to name names.

Miller wasn't done yet, either. Not by a long shot.

"So, you want to know the funniest part?" he said. "First, Jeanne made Jared tell on himself, and then she turned right around and dumped him."

"She...what?"

"Dumped him," he said. "Just like that."

And I thought—

So, in other words, the only thing that could have possibly topped everything else that day—did.

Jeanne dumped Jared.

Jared had locked me in the bathroom.

Miller hadn't.

"But…wait," I said. "So, when Mrs. Stricker took roll call—"

Miller shrugged. "Yeah, that's on me. Kind of force of habit, you know?"

"Right, but then why didn't you *say* anything?" I asked.

"I just thought you were sitting somewhere else," Miller told me. "They figured it out before I did."

"Dude!"

"I'm not your babysitter, idiot."

It was like the end of the longest day ever. By now, I just wanted to stop talking, go to bed, and try to figure out what it all meant before my brain turned into potted meat.

But first, I had one more thing to do.

"Hey, Miller," I said.

He wasn't paying attention anymore. He was

demolishing a bag of chips and watching darts on TV like it was the most interesting thing ever. (It's not.)

I kept going anyway.

"I'm going to sleep out here tonight," I said, pointing at the other bed. "I'm kind of sick of that bathtub."

"Whatever," Miller said, flicking some salt-and-vinegar crumbs on the floor. "But I get the remote, and we turn out the lights when I say so."

"Yeah, okay," I said.

I could live with that. No problem.

BRAIN STRAIN

The next morning started off like Christmas. It was our last day in London, and when I got on the bus, Jared wasn't on it.

I guess they took his whole prank thing pretty seriously. I heard people talking about how he was being held back at the hotel all day. Not only that, but Mrs. Stricker was the one staying with him.

So like I said, Merry Christmas to me!

Mostly, though, I couldn't stop thinking about Jeanne. We were on our way to visit an English middle school, and I kept trying to figure out how to talk to her on that bus ride.

But it was no use. Ever since she broke up with Jared, her friends had been sticking to her like some kind of all-girl security detail. There was no way I'd be busting through that perimeter anytime soon.

I've never been the most confident kid this side of the sun. Still, I kept wondering if Jeanne might be thinking about me at least a little bit.

I know. That's crazy, right? A complete waste of brain space (that I could be using on math or something useful). So then why was I thinking it?

Because I couldn't help it, I guess. It was like this giant tug-of-war, back and forth, back and forth, inside my head.

By the time we got to the school, it was like an exact tie, and I still wasn't any closer to knowing what I should do.

What I *really* needed was another one of those signs. Maybe a billboard this time—something to tell me what to say and when to say it.

But in the meantime, the day was just getting started and my brain was ready for a nap.

I couldn't take too much more of this. Something had to give soon.

And in fact, I didn't know it yet, but something would.

Even sooner than I thought.

Does Jeanne Like Me (LIKE THAT)?
Jared was acting jealous.
Jeanne and I have this cool, secret partnership.
Leo's right. I need to tell her how I feel.
Hey, I think she just looked at me!

OF COURSE NOT, YOU IDIOT!
So what?
That's for school, dummy.
Stand by to get laughed at!
Dream on!

THE SAME BUT DIFFERENT

We walked in the door of Bealing Bright Secondary School.

"Please proceed to your host group and get to know one another as we begin our day together," some English guy kept going. "We have a fun morning planned for all!"

The first thing they did was divide us into smaller groups and show us all around the school.

That part was just okay, to be honest. We'd already taken about eighty tours that week, and I was all toured out. Also, Jeanne wasn't in my group.

After that, everyone got buddied up with one of the English students. I got some kid named Abdullah, and I was supposed to follow his schedule and see what a "typical" day was like for him.

It was cool at first, just hanging out at the lockers and meeting some of his friends. I learned some more new words, too. Or at least new ways to use them, like *brilliant,* and *wally,* and *quid*. There were some others, but I don't know if I'm allowed to say them here. (Question: Are bad British words still bad when you say them in the United States? I'm not sure, but I'm not taking any chances, either.)

After that, I went to Abdullah's classes with him, starting with history, where the teacher talked for a long time about the causes and consequences of the Industrial Revolution, and... zzzzzzzzzz.

See? I can't even tell you about that part

without falling asleep. It turns out that the biggest lesson I learned was that English middle school was just as boring as American middle school.

But then just before lunch, a bunch of us got to go outside for a while.

"What do you say, guys?" Abdullah asked us. "Up for a little football?"

"Yes!" Miller said.

"You know they mean soccer, right?" I said.

"Oh," Miller said. "Then whatever." But he played anyway.

I'm not exactly a world-class soccer player. I'm not even a Hills Village–class soccer player. But it was all pretty friendly. They didn't even make us line up and get picked (or not picked) one at a time. Which was cool.

They put Miller in as goalie on my team. I guess that was because he took up more space in the goal than anybody. He definitely looked ready to tackle whatever came his way, and I wondered if he still remembered it wasn't regular football.

I got put at left fullback. That meant I was on defense, which was better than being on the front line. Most of those English guys played like they were born with soccer balls attached to their toes.

The problem was, I'm not left-footed. So I was always running up to the ball, twisting around, and trying to kick with the outside of my right foot. Which looked just about as goofy as it sounds. I'm pretty sure I was giving soccer *and* America a bad name at the same time.

On top of all that, they had another game going on the next field. And that's where I finally spotted Jeanne again. Once I saw her, it was hard to stop looking over there. I could have watched her play soccer all day.

But then I realized someone was shouting from much closer by. And they weren't just shouting *near* me. They were shouting *at* me.

"WAKE UP, KHATCHADORIAN!"

It was Miller. And when I looked around, I saw why. The other team's front line was coming our way. They'd just gotten past the midfielders, which left us fullbacks as the last line of defense.

I totally should have focused then, but I couldn't help taking one more look at the other field. I wanted to see if Jeanne was watching.

And this time, she was. In fact, she was looking

right at me. That's when she waved. And even smiled! Which seemed like a good sign.

A very good sign.

So at least she wasn't ignoring me. She probably just had other stuff on her mind that morning. Which I could totally understand. Maybe that even meant—

"KHATCHADORIAN!" Miller yelled again.

This time when I looked back, I had the world's biggest English kid practically on top of me. In fact, he'd just taken a shot.

The last thing I saw was that soccer ball coming straight at my face.

The good news? I managed to stop the ball from going into the goal.

The bad news? I stopped it with my face.

To celebrate, I spun around, fell over, and hit the dirt like a hundred pounds of dead American weight.

RECOVERY ROOM

So imagine getting punched in the nose. Got it? Now imagine if your whole head was just one big nose.

That's about what it felt like when that ball hit my face.

I didn't pass out or anything. It was more like someone shut down the power station that ran my brain for a few seconds. Everything kind of went blurry, then dark, then back to blurry again.

"You okay?" someone said.

"Ye-ahh," I said. I was still facedown, sniffing the grass, and I didn't *feel* okay, but it seemed like the right thing to say.

"Watch out, lads," some adult called out. Then I felt a hand on my arm. "Not to worry, son. You're all right."

I recognized his voice. It was the guy who made all the announcements that morning, Mr. Covington. He was the assistant headmaster, which I think is British for vice principal.

"Can you roll over?" he asked me.

"I think so," I said. But when I did, it was like suddenly *I* was the scary movie and all of them were the audience.

I guess that ball turned my nose on like a faucet, and my face looked something like a cheese-free pizza by then. My shirt was all splotchy red, too.

"Oh…my," Mr. Covington said. He handed me a handkerchief from his pocket, but without exactly looking at me. I don't think he liked all that blood.

"Let's get him inside, boys," he said, and a couple of the other guys got me on my feet. Then they all walked me over to Mr. Covington's office and put me in a chair with my head back.

Ms. Donatello was there now, too, and she cleaned me up while Mr. Covington kept busy intensely *not* looking at me. Instead, he got on the PA and made another announcement.

"Attention, ladies and gentlemen. Our American patient is doing just fine," he said. "We expect a full recovery in no time."

I could hear some people clapping down the hall then, which was cool. Seriously, these were like the nicest kids I'd ever met. I was starting to think maybe I should move to England and go to school here instead of going back to HVMS.

"How about some ice?" Ms. D said.

“Sure,” I said, except it sounded like *“Chure”* because of all the toilet paper in my nose.

“I’ll go with you!” Mr. Covington said. “We’ll see about finding Rafe another shirt.”

That was okay with me. Mr. C was making me nervous, anyway. So I just stayed there, kept my head back, and waited for my face to stop aching.

I wasn’t alone for long. A second later, I heard the door open, and I thought, *That was quick*. But when I looked up, it wasn’t Ms. D, or Mr. C, or the ice, or a new shirt, or any of those things.

Not even close, in fact.

This time, it was Jeanne.

THREE (OR MORE LIKE SEVEN) LITTLE WORDS

"Can I come in?" Jeanne asked.

"Chure," I said.

I couldn't say no to Jeanne about anything, even if I wanted to. And I *didn't* want to. I was too busy thinking, *WOW! IF THIS ISN'T A SIGN, I DON'T KNOW WHAT IS.*

"Rafe, I am *so* sorry!" Jeanne said. "I shouldn't have waved like that. I feel like this was all my fault."

It totally *wasn't* her fault, of course. It was my own fault. I was the one who couldn't stop staring at her. But try admitting that one out loud. Hopeless!

"Don't worry aboud id," I told her smoothly. Oh right, the toilet-paper nose plugs—not a good look when talking to the girl of your dreams. I turned away for a second and yanked them out, hoping the bleeding had stopped.

"I heard you were doing okay," she went on with concern in her voice.

"Yeah, I think everyone heard that," I said. Jeanne laughed, which made me laugh, but that hurt my nose, so I stopped.

Then she sat down on the edge of the desk. I could tell she didn't want to come too close. But she wasn't leaving, either.

"What about you?" I said. "How are *you* doing?"

"I'm okay," she said. "I guess that means you heard about me and Jared."

"Yeah," I said. I was sitting up now. My nose

wasn't dripping blood anymore. That was good, even if it wasn't as romantic as a kiss in the pouring rain or two Shakespearean kids dying in a crypt somewhere.

"So, um…speaking of all that," I said. "I kind of wanted to talk to you about something kinda important."

"You did?" Jeanne said. "What?"

Oh man. Here it comes.

Was I really going to do this?

Yeah. I really was.

Really really?

Yeah. *Really* really.

I took a deep breath.

"It's just that…you've been so great about the whole report and everything. I really appreciate it," I told her.

"Don't worry about it," Jeanne said.

"Well, it's not just that," I said. "It's more like…I just wanted to say…I think if you liked me half as much as I like you, I'd be pretty amazed. I'd be flabbergasted, actually."

"Don't be silly," she said. "I wouldn't be helping you if I didn't like you."

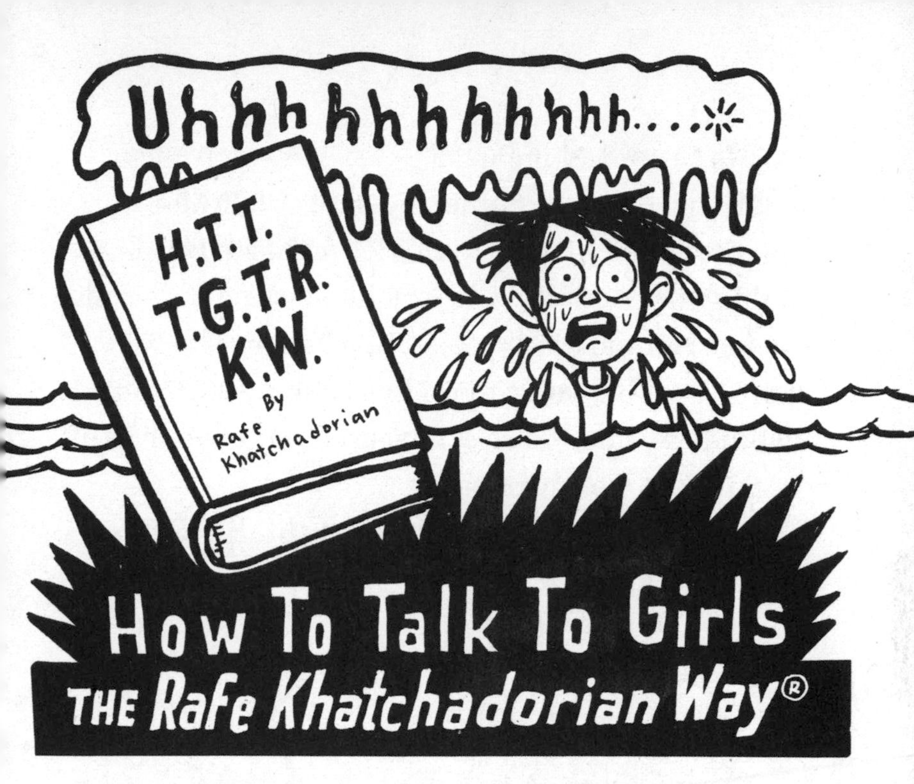

How To Talk To Girls
THE *Rafe Khatchadorian Way*®

CHAPTER 1: Me, Myself, And I Am Such An Idiot

CHAPTER 2: Confused? Get Used To It

CHAPTER 3: Blindsided! How To Mess Up And Not Even Know It

CHAPTER 4: Love Means Always Having To Say You're Sorry

CHAPTER 5: You Know What? Maybe You Should Ask Someone Else

CHAPTER 6: Seriously, Why Are You Still Reading This?

CHAPTER 7: Just So You Know, The Rest Of This Book Is Blank

400 PAGES! BUY NOW!

"No," I said. "I mean..."

My heart was hammering, and it felt like breathing had just gotten twice as hard. But I couldn't back out now. It was like sitting on a roller coaster right after it takes off, when you know there's nothing you can do to stop it even if you wanted to—but you're still scared out of your skull.

So I just went with it.

"What I mean is," I told her, "I think I kind of, uh, *love* you."

So it wasn't exactly what I meant to say. But it wasn't exactly a lie, either. At least, I don't think it was. I don't really know what love is supposed to feel like. All I know is that when I opened my big fat mouth, those are the words that came out: *I think I kind of love you*. No taking them back now.

Two seconds passed by in silence, but it felt like two hours. She eventually had to say something, right? Something that was probably going to change my life forever. Something either really painful or really phenomenal. Something like...

"Oh," Jeanne said.

Oh.

Which felt like a big fist through my heart.

"I guess that was a pretty stupid thing to say," I said in a rush. I didn't know what else to do besides crawl into the corner and wish I could disappear.

"No it wasn't," Jeanne said just as quickly. "It's just, I didn't mean for you to think...I mean, I didn't break up with Jared because...I mean, I didn't come in here to—"

Just then the door opened again, and Mr. Covington came flying in. A bag of ice dropped out of his hand, slid across the floor, and landed under my chair. But he didn't seem to notice.

"Excuse me, young lady," he said, taking Jeanne by the arm.

"I'm sorry!" she said, getting on her feet. "I know I'm not supposed to be in here—"

"No, it's not that," he said. "It's *that.*" And he pointed down at the desk, where the PA system was. With the microphone. And the talk button. The one Jeanne had been sitting on until just a second ago.

Jeanne's eyes got huge.

"You mean...," she said.

Mr. Covington kind of sighed, with an expression like he felt sorry for us both.

"I'm afraid so," he said.

I could see some people out in the hall now. They were looking into the room and whispering to each other. Some of them were laughing, too. Not in the good way.

And that's when I started thinking maybe it was time for me to leave that school, ASAP.

And London.

And England.

And Planet Earth, too, if I had anything to say about it.

CHAPTER 55

FRIENDS, I GUESS

Mr. Covington gave me the ice for my nose and a Bealing Bright Secondary School T-shirt to wear. Then he kind of backed out the door and said he'd give us "a moment."

Jeanne was really nice about the whole thing after that. Of course.

And it helped. Some.

But I still felt like I'd made the biggest bonehead move of my life. Which is saying a lot, for me.

"I'm sorry, Rafe," Jeanne said awkwardly. She paused and then continued. "Well, I bet you'll have a girlfriend soon anyway. I know Sabra and Katrina both think you're cute."

"Sure, in a dorky way," I said.

"You don't know that," she said.

"Actually, I do," I said. Now it sounded like I was feeling sorry for myself. "Don't worry about it," I said.

"Well, please don't take it personally, Rafe. I mean, I *just* broke up with Jared," she said.

"Yeah, but still. You're not saying there might be a chance," I said, weakly smiling to make her feel a little better. "Or are you?"

"Well…no," she told me. "I guess not."

"That's okay," I said.

Jeanne's always told me the truth about everything. I wasn't going to hold this one against her, even if it did feel like my heart had just taken its own soccer ball to the face.

"So, I hope it's okay to ask this," Jeanne said, "but is there any chance you'd want to be friends now? Like, for real?"

"Seriously?" I said.

"Yeah," Jeanne said. "We really do make a good team, Rafe. Just not...you know. Like that."

I didn't know *what* I wanted just then. I mean, I know guys and girls can be friends, no problem. But what about a guy who just told a girl "I think I kind of love you" while the whole world listened in? Can *they* be friends?

Maybe not.

But I guess I was going to find out. Because like I said before, I couldn't say no to Jeanne about anything. Including this.

But I did have one other question.

"What about Jared?" I said. "He knows everything. Isn't he going to tell Mrs. Stricker about the whole secret partner thing?"

Jeanne shook her head. "To tell you the truth, I don't think he wants to make me any madder than he did yesterday," she said. Then she stuck out her hand. "So anyway—friends?"

"Chure," I said.

And we shook on it. Again.

CHAPTER 56

SHOWDOWN iN ROOM 568

I guess I *could* tell you about how much everyone stared at me when I came out of that office. And how much they talked about me on the bus. And laughed at me all the way back to the hotel.

But I'm not going to. I mean, you get the idea, right? If I told you about every single time I got laughed at, you'd be reading my story into the next century.

So let's just skip to the next part.

When we got to the hotel, the chaperones told us all to pack our bags and be down in the lobby at four o'clock sharp. It was time to go home.

So I was packing, and Miller went to take a shower. There was a knock at the door, so it was on me to go answer.

I guess I should have used the peephole or asked who it was, but I didn't think about it. Not until—

BLAM!

As soon as I cracked that door, Jared was inside the room. And he was moving in for the kill, too. I could see it in his eyes. He'd heard about everything that had happened at the school that morning.

"You're the reason she broke up with me!" he said.

"No I'm not!" I sputtered.

The truth was, Jeanne broke up with Jared because of Jared. But I wasn't going to tell him that.

"You've been planning this all along," he said. "And now you're going to pay!"

I'm not exactly afraid of fighting. But I *was* afraid of what would happen if I did—starting with Jared's fists and ending with Mrs. Stricker.

So I jumped up on the nearest bed to get out of the way, then down to the other side.

"Stop running and take it!" Jared said. He came around, but I jumped back up on the mattress and—*BOING!*—straight over to the next bed.

Jared dove and tried to cut me off. I jumped back the other way, then down onto the floor by the window. When he came at me again, I jumped up, across, over, and down again, like some kind of crazed kangaroo.

"QUIT IT!" he said.

"You first!" I said.

He made a grab for me again and I jumped to the far bed.

It was getting beyond stupid. Right up until—

"What's going on out here?!" Miller yelled, with a towel around his waist.

Jared stopped cold. I did, too. It was like some weird game of freeze tag, but with way higher stakes.

"No offense, Miller," Jared said, "but mind your own business. This is between me and Rafe."

"Yeah, well..." Miller walked out into the middle of the room, with his hair dripping the whole way. "Now *I'm* between you and Rafe. Got it?"

"Give me a break," Jared said. "You've wanted to kick his butt since the beginning of middle school."

"Been there, done that," Miller said. "Trust me, it's not that hard."

"Gee, thanks," I said.

"Shut up, Rafe," he said. "So, Jared, as I was saying…GET OUT OF OUR ROOM!"

Even though the situation was beyond crazy, I took a sec to appreciate that Miller called it "our" room. We'd come a long way from him cleaning his toenails with my toothbrush.

Anyway, by now Miller was looming so close to Jared that he was dripping water right on top of him. Jared was backing toward the door.

"Whatever," he said.

The thing is, Jared's bigger than me, but Miller's bigger than everyone. It was pretty clear by now that I'd already spilled all the blood I was going to spill that day.

I don't know if you can call that a lucky break or not. But what I do know is that Miller the Killer takes the world's fastest showers.

I've never been so grateful for someone's bad hygiene in my life.

HOME, HOME ON THE RANGE

So I made it out of that hotel room alive. And back across the Atlantic Ocean without screwing up again, too.

Life is getting back to whatever it's getting back to now. I can't say "normal" because my life is never normal. But it's good to be home again. The class trip did cause a few big changes, but for now you can just put them on the long list of stuff I'll never understand.

As for Jared, it's not exactly over yet. It's more like

things are on pause for a few weeks. That's when Miller's leaving town and moving to Phoenix. In the meantime, the kid formerly known as Miller the Killer is now my unofficial bodyguard. How crazy is *that?*

I learned a lot in London. And one of those things is that Miller isn't so bad after all. Not once you get to know him a little, get tortured by him for a few years, and then get to know him a little more. If he weren't moving away, we might have even gotten to be friends. Which is something I never, ever, ever, ever, ever, ever, ever...

...ever, ever, ever...

...*ever* thought I'd say.

But I guess that's how it goes. When life closes a Miller-sized door, it opens up a Jared-shaped window. Which means I'm getting ready for a whole new kind of battle. So stay tuned on that one, and wish me luck. I think I'm going to need it.

Things with me and Jeanne are different now, too. And you might not believe this, but I'm not completely sorry I told her about...you know what. (Don't make me say it again.) Like, I'm obviously sorry about the PA mic being on at the worst

possible time, but things aren't so bad now.

See, all that stuff with Jeanne was like this giant weight I'd been holding on to since the very first time I saw her. And even though I basically dropped it on my foot when I put it down, I also don't have to carry it around anymore.

And guess what else? Jeanne wasn't kidding when she said we made a good team. We actually put together a whole movie night to show our families and everyone else at school what we did in London. People put up posters and printouts of their mini-modules and all the pictures they took, and everyone's parents came to see it. Then we all sat down in the library and watched the videos on a big screen, too.

They could have just seen that stuff online, but Jeanne thought it would be cool to have a screening party. Ms. Donatello thought so, too, and helped make it all happen. We had popcorn and drinks, and everyone applauded at the end.

And it *was* cool. Really cool. Especially seeing how much they all liked those videos. I'm not going to say they were *mine,* exactly, because it really was a group project.

But between you and me and Leo the Silent? I think I made a pretty good Artist in Chief.

I also made a new friend in London, like Mom said I should try to do. Or maybe it was more like a new friend and a half, if you count what happened with Miller. So it turned out that I followed Mom's advice after all. Just not in the way I ever expected to.

Which I guess is my new version of normal.

I DON'T KNOW ABOUT HONORABLE, BUT I'LL TAKE THE MENTION

P.S. I know you've been wondering. And the answer is *sort of.*

We didn't win first place in that Living-Learning Contest. There were over two hundred entries, and some school from Oregon snagged the win without even leaving the U.S. (They did the Grand Canyon.)

But the good news is, those contest people also gave out twenty-five honorable mentions. And GUESS WHO GOT ONE?

Hills Village Middle School, that's who! When they sent the letter to the school, it said, "The judging panel was particularly impressed with your creative video additions to the standard report."

Yeah, my head swelled up a little bit about that. Just a little, anyway.

Not only that, but every honorable mention came with a hundred-dollar prize. It was supposed to go into a random drawing, but everyone from our trip voted and gave it to me, if you can believe that. (I'm pretty sure it wasn't a unanimous vote. Right, Jared?)

So maybe I didn't win a thousand bucks, but I did win a hundred, which was awesome. Even if it got cut down to fifty dollars after I shared it with Jeanne. And then down to $42.29 when we went to Bosco's to split a pizza and talk about what our next project is going to be.

I'm thinking giant blockbuster action film. She's thinking of expanding the online school newspaper, with more articles and art and videos. We haven't exactly decided yet.

But if we ever *do* start cranking out huge, mega-successful movies, then I know exactly what our company's going to be called.

Because like I said before, Jeanne has the

brains and I have the creativity. She's got the friends to help out, and I've got...a few more friends than I had before. She has good ideas spilling out of her brain, and I have a few leaking out of mine.

So watch out, world. We're just getting started here.

You haven't seen anything yet!

LIVE
Thank You, Thank You, Thank You!
RAFE K.
I'd like to thank Jeanne Galletta, and everyone else on our team...
WE DID IT!
HVMS

LIVE
WINNER
HONORABLE
MENTION
My family... my teachers
...the Academy...
Rafe Khatchadorian
HONORABLE MENTION
Sometimes
a sign
is just
a sign.
phoenix
or
BUST
WALK
ME!!

JAMES PATTERSON received the Literarian Award for Outstanding Service to the American Literary Community from the National Book Foundation. He holds the Guinness World Record for the most #1 *New York Times* bestsellers, including *Middle School*, *I Funny*, and *Jacky Ha-Ha*, and his books have sold more than 350 million copies worldwide. A tireless champion of the power of books and reading, Patterson created a children's book imprint, JIMMY Patterson, whose mission is simple: "We want every kid who finishes a JIMMY Book to say, 'PLEASE GIVE ME ANOTHER BOOK.'" He has donated more than one million books to students and soldiers and funds over four hundred Teacher Education Scholarships at twenty-four colleges and universities. He has also donated millions of dollars to independent bookstores and school libraries. Patterson invests proceeds from the sales of JIMMY Patterson Books in pro-reading initiatives.

CHRIS TEBBETTS has collaborated with James Patterson on eight other books in the Middle School series as well as *Public School Superhero*, and is also the author of The Viking, a fantasy adventure series for young readers. He lives in Vermont.

LAURA PARK is a cartoonist and the illustrator of four books in the I Funny series and six books in the Middle School series. She is the author of the minicomic series *Do Not Disturb My Waking Dream,* and her work has appeared in *The Best American Comics*. She lives in Chicago.

IT'S TIME FOR
MIDDLE SCHOOL!

My name is
Rafe Khatchadorian,
and if there's one thing I know,
it's how to stay out of trouble.
JUST KIDDING!
If you're in ~~jail~~ middle school,
you'll laugh your butt off reading
about all my crazy adventures!

RAAAA-AAFE!!

READ ALL OF MY BOOKS, AVAILABLE NOW!

MIDDLE SCHOOL THE WORST YEARS OF MY LIFE
JAMES PATTERSON AND CHRIS TEBBETTS
MIDDLE SCHOOL GET ME OUT OF HERE!
JAMES PATTERSON AND CHRIS TEBBETTS
MIDDLE SCHOOL BIG FAT LIAR
JAMES PATTERSON AND LISA PAPADEMETRIOU
MIDDLE SCHOOL HOW I SURVIVED BULLIES, BROCCOLI, AND SNAKE HILL
JAMES PATTERSON AND CHRIS TEBBETTS
MIDDLE SCHOOL ULTIMATE SHOWDOWN
JAMES PATTERSON AND JULIA BERGEN
MIDDLE SCHOOL SAVE RAFE!
JAMES PATTERSON AND CHRIS TEBBETTS
MIDDLE SCHOOL Just My Rotten Luck
JAMES PATTERSON AND CHRIS TEBBETTS
NEW MIDDLE SCHOOL DOG'S BEST FRIEND
JAMES PATTERSON AND CHRIS TEBBETTS
NEW MIDDLE SCHOOL ESCAPE TO AUSTRALIA
JAMES PATTERSON AND MARTIN CHATTERTON
MIDDLE SCHOOL FROM HERO TO ZERO
JAMES PATTERSON AND CHRIS TEBBETTS